Dear God, he'd kissed her...

Any self-control Jeremiah could have used to pull away dissipated when she leaned into the kiss, her tongue sliding against his, sending tendrils of heat through his entire body.

Before he could deepen the kiss, though, she pulled away. Her breath was heavy and her eyes wide, and he realized what had just happened.

"That was so bad," she moaned.

He grimaced. "The kiss was bad?" he asked, unable to help himself.

She shook her head even more furiously. "The kiss was too good. That's what makes it so bad."

"So you liked the kiss?"

She looked at him through her fingers. "That's not helping. There's no way we can do that again. Jessica will flip if she finds out."

"I'm not going to tell her about it. Are you?"

"No way," Renee responded immediately.

"So," Jeremiah said slowly, picking his words with care, "if neither of us tells her, and she doesn't see us, is there any reason why we can't do it again?"

Dear Reader,

So much has changed since my first book, *Her Sexy Vegas Cowboy*, was published: my husband and I started traveling full-time; we welcomed our sweet baby, Annabelle, into the world; and I completed my second Harlequin novel, which you hold in your hands. Quite a bit of it was typed one-handed on a phone while caring for a newborn. Lucky for me, she was a pretty good sport about the whole thing and let me bounce ideas off her.

Once I finished *Her Sexy Vegas Cowboy*, it was clear that Jeremiah would need his own story; with his humor and constant optimism, he's my kind of hero, and I wanted to hear more from him and whether or not he would ever find his own happily-ever-after. In addition, the first "fan" email I received from a reader (shout-out to Caitlin!) asked if I was planning on writing a book about him.

I struggled with this book at first, though. I wasn't sure who the heroine was or where the story would be set. After going through a lot of (bad) ideas, I realized the story had to happen right before Jessica and Aaron's Texas wedding, and then it became obvious who Jeremiah would fall for—the sister of the bride. After that, everything fell into place.

The antics of Renee and Jeremiah made me smile, giggle and sigh. I hope it is the same for you and that you enjoy reading about these two as much as I enjoyed writing about them.

Cheers,

Ali Olson

Ali Olson

Her Sexy Texas Cowboy

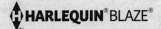

Recycling programs
for this product may
not exist in your area.

ISBN-13: 978-0-373-79955-8

Her Sexy Texas Cowboy

Copyright © 2017 by Mary Olson

Printed in U.S.A.

www.Harlequin.com

Ali Olson is a longtime resident of Las Vegas, Nevada, where she has been teaching English at the high school and college level for the past seven years. Ali has found a passion for writing sexy romance novels, both contemporary and historical, and is enthusiastic about her newly discovered career. She loves reading, writing and traveling with her husband and constant companion, Joe. She appreciates hearing from readers. Write to her at authoraliolson.com.

Books by Ali Olson

Harlequin Blaze

Her Sexy Vegas Cowboy

To get the inside scoop on Harlequin Blaze and its talented writers, be sure to check out BlazeAuthors.com.

All backlist available in ebook format.

Visit the Author Profile page at Harlequin.com for more titles.

For my baby girl, Annabelle. You're going to read this one day. That's going to be a very weird day.

1

"JESSICA, IT'LL ALL be fine. You just need to stop worrying," Renee said in her most soothing voice, trying to calm her sister's newest anxiety issue. She couldn't help but roll her eyes, though, and was glad her sister couldn't see her through the phone.

"I know you're rolling your eyes at me over there," her sister chirped back, "but this is *important*. What if the whole thing is a disaster? I've been planning for months for every possible problem, but I never expected this."

Renee sighed. "Stew is a nice guy. You're just freaking out because you haven't met him yet and it's a little weird to think of Mom having a boyfriend. What do you think he'll do, scream obscenities during the ceremony? Take off all his clothes and bathe in the potato salad at the reception?"

She snorted, picturing her mother's slightly stuffy boyfriend doing anything of the sort. "Besides," she continued, "I thought your wedding was going to be super low-key. You're having it at your house. How much could there possibly be to plan, or to screw up? You said you were keeping it casual."

She looked at the bridesmaid's dress hanging on the back of her door. It was all clean lines and conservative cuts. Pretty, but definitely not something she would wear to a gala or anything. The only thing that kept it from being something Renee might wear to a dinner with friends—besides the fact that she was always too busy to go to dinner with friends—was the color: a gorgeous violet, the color of a summer evening right after the sun set.

It was a beautiful color, but Renee knew it was all wrong for her. She pushed her shoulder-length, strawberry blond hair behind her right ear, wishing she'd been gifted with Jessica's lustrous auburn locks. Her sister could pull off that color just fine, but Renee was certain it just made her look even more washed-out and freckly than normal. Not that she'd say anything like that to her worrier of a sister.

"It's casual," Jessica replied, "just a very *planned* casual. I don't want to have to worry about anything that day, and the only way that'll happen is if I have everything planned. That way, I won't need to feel anxious about anything."

"That's why I'm flying in tomorrow, Jess. I'm tying up the last few things at work tomorrow morning, and then I'll have the whole week completely free to help with everything. We'll make sure it's all ready and you can enjoy the weekend without needing to triple-check anything, because we'll have already taken care of it."

Renee waited for her sister to see the logic in what she said, though she seriously doubted Jessica's ability to go an entire day, *especially* her wedding day, without feeling anxious. Still, it was her job to keep her sister from freaking out, and she was prepared to do her damnedest. No matter how difficult it was for her to go an entire week away from her job.

She heard Jessica let out a deep breath and smiled to herself. After twenty-six years as sisters, she'd gotten pretty good at figuring out how Jessica was feeling, and she knew she'd said the right thing.

"You're right, Renee. It'll be great, I'm sure. Thanks again for coming down early and helping. I owe you."

"It's nothing," she answered, even though her fingers itched when she thought of all the work she'd be missing over the next week. "I have the vacation time just sitting there, and we can spend some time doing sisterly things. It's been a long while since just the two of us hung out." Renee picked up another pair of jeans and tossed them into her half-filled suitcase.

"Definitely. Oh! I almost forgot. Is it okay if Aaron's friend Jeremiah picks you up from the airport? He's going to be in town anyway. You remember him from Vegas, right?"

Renee felt her ears burn, so glad her sister couldn't see her blush. She remembered Jeremiah, all right. Her heart thumped harder in her chest just thinking about Aaron's drop-dead-gorgeous friend. She had flown to Las Vegas in early December to surprise her sister with her perfect "bachelorette party," which meant dinner and drinks with family and Jessica's best friend, Cindy.

Renee hadn't expected to be introduced to the sexiest man she'd ever met, but when Jeremiah walked in with Jessica's fiancé, she nearly fell out of her chair. Even over a month later, she could still picture his sparkling brown eyes, easy smile and thick dark hair, which she had spent more time than she'd like to admit imagining running her fingers through. The blood rushed away from her face and to a much more intimate location just thinking about it.

"Renee?"

She was brought abruptly out of her reverie by her sister's voice. "Sure, that's fine," she responded, hoping her sister didn't notice her sudden breathlessness.

"Great. He said he'd meet you at baggage claim. See you tomorrow, little sis. Thanks again."

"Love ya, big sis. See you tomorrow."

She hung up and sat at her table, letting her mind wander right back to Jeremiah. She hadn't really talked to him that night in Vegas, and that was on purpose. Throwing herself at the best friend of her sister's soon-to-be husband was definitely a no-no, and trying to have a normal conversation with someone that sexy seemed impossible. Avoiding the situation altogether had been her only plan of action.

Still, she couldn't help but notice how friendly and easygoing he was with the whole group. She also couldn't help but notice the way his muscles moved under his shirt and the way his lips begged to be kissed. He had been playing the starring role in her fantasies since then, and those lips had played a *very* important part.

And now she was going to be spending a significant

amount of time with him in close quarters. She gave herself about a fifty percent chance of getting through the car ride without saying or doing something incredibly stupid.

Renee shook her head, trying to get herself together. This week was about Jessica and Aaron, not her desire to jump into bed with Jeremiah. Maybe if she told herself that enough times, she'd remember it when she actually saw him.

JEREMIAH'S EYES, THE color of coffee, captured her and sent jolts of excitement along her spine. He stepped so close she could feel the heat from his body all the way down hers, and he placed his hand on her neck, his thumb rubbing along her jawline, making her purr in response.

His other arm slid around her waist, pulling her even closer, until her body was pressed against his and she could feel his hardness and strength. Renee let her hands graze over the muscles of his arms as they moved up and around his neck.

When he spoke, his voice was a low growl, his usual carefree tones darkened with primal urgency. "You have no idea how long I've wanted to do this."

Her breath came in short gasps as she waited while he leaned toward her with agonizing slowness, his lips drawing ever closer. Her mouth opened for him, inviting him in.

Renee sighed and opened her eyes. Her dark bedroom greeted her, feeling much colder and emptier than it usually did. She glanced at her phone for the time and groaned. Her alarm would be going off in five minutes. Not nearly enough time to slip back into her dream and enjoy the image as completely as she would like.

She told herself to get up, but stayed under the covers with her eyes closed, allowing the picture to last just another moment.

Finally, after another sigh, she pulled herself out of bed and turned on the light, running her fingers over her face and through the tangles of her hair. She hadn't seen Jeremiah in weeks, yet she could still picture exactly how sexy he was. And if she couldn't keep her hands off him in her dreams, how was she possibly going to get through the next week around him?

Maybe he wasn't as fantastic in real life, she told herself. Maybe she'd let her imagination run away with her since Vegas, and he'd end up being a complete disappointment when she saw him again.

Yeah, right.

She shook her head to quiet her thoughts and tried to refocus her mind on the tasks she wanted to tackle this morning, but even her job couldn't completely erase the image of Jeremiah with his arm encircling her. She shook her head again and went to make some coffee. It was going to be a long day.

FORTY MINUTES LATER, Renee walked through the snowy streets to work. It was only a couple of blocks from her apartment, but her toes felt frozen by the time she stepped into the building, and she gratefully breathed in the blast of hot air that greeted her. New York City was bitterly cold in February, and her dress slacks and heels didn't exactly keep her toasty. At least Texas would be warmer, she reminded herself, trying to create some excitement about her trip to replace her nerves over seeing Jeremiah again and the guilt of being away from her job for so long.

In the elevator, she took off her thick coat and brushed her hair back off her shoulders, watching the numbers climb until it stopped on the twentieth floor. As the doors slid open, the two-foot-high letters loomed above her, as they did every day, and just like every other day, they made her smile. The *Empire Magazine* head office had been her home for almost four years, since she became an intern fresh out of college, and she felt her heart jump with excitement in the same way it had since her first day.

Renee's friends constantly told her she was a workaholic and needed to take a break, but the truth was, she loved her job. She had meant to take today off as well as next week, but in the end she hadn't been able to do it—there were a few last things she wanted to tweak before going, and Renee couldn't bring herself to leave the work for the others on her team. Or worse, just submit everything as it was.

Striding quickly through the hallways, Renee made her way to her office, smiling at coworkers as she went.

As her computer booted to life, she settled into her chair. She just needed two hours to finish perfecting one of her spreads for the next issue, and then she would leave, she promised herself.

A head covered in black curls popped into her doorway as Jeff, a man on Renee's design team, leaned in.

"You're not supposed to be here, remember? That's how vacations work."

Renee smiled. "I know. I'm just not quite finished with the layout of one of my articles. Then I'll go, I promise. I've got a flight to catch."

"Well, Patty heard you were in the office. She wants to see you, whenever you have a second."

She thanked him, wondering what her boss could possibly want to see her about. She was probably just going to lecture her about overworking again. Patty did that every few weeks, and had been overjoyed when Renee told her she needed to use some of her vacation time.

Renee glanced at her computer once more before leaving her office. The spreads would need to wait a few more minutes.

Four hours later, Renee rushed out of the building into the icy air, praying she would make her flight. Her mind was such a jumble with what Patty had told her that there was hardly any room for anxiety to creep in.

After forty years in the business, Patty was retiring. And she wanted Renee to take over her position. Renee still couldn't believe it. She had thought it would be years before she'd get this opportunity, and here it was, so close she could taste it.

As she hopped out of the cab and dashed into the airport, thoughts of her new job stuck with her, sending flurries of excitement through her stomach.

Or maybe that was from the thoughts of Jeremiah, who would be waiting for her when she landed Texas. He hadn't been far from her thoughts the whole morning, either.

2

JEREMIAH PARKED HIS truck in the concrete structure outside of the airport. He was glad Renee's plane wouldn't be landing for another fifteen minutes, because he needed some time to pull himself together and calm down. Not that he'd been able to do that all day, or really since he'd met her in Vegas weeks ago.

For the thousandth time, he reminded himself that this was Jessica's little sister and he'd have to be an idiot to even try to make something happen with her, no matter how fast his blood surged through him when he pictured her. He'd spent enough time around Jessica since she moved down to Texas from New York to know exactly how badly it would go if he made a move on Renee.

Not that he and Jessica didn't get along, but dating someone in her family was a whole different story. He knew just how protective Jessica was about her little sister, and he was pretty sure Jessica thought of him as some kind of pickup artist. Not the kind of guy you'd want your sister with.

He could only imagine what Jessica had told Renee about him. Even if she wasn't off-limits, the chance that she'd be interested was slim enough. She probably thought he was a playboy who spent the majority of his time flirting with random strangers. Which, he had to admit, wasn't far from the truth for the majority of his adult life. But he was almost thirty now, and for the past year or so the excitement of that life had dwindled and died.

And then he met Renee, who put the final nails in that coffin without even knowing it. She had passed into and out of his life like a breath of fresh air, making the prospects of other women seem dull and stale in comparison.

He didn't even know what it was about her that had struck him so forcefully, but he'd been knocked backward when he first saw her. Their first night in Vegas, he and Aaron and Jessica had gone to dinner with her bachelorette party, which consisted of Jessica's best friend, sister and mother. The moment they entered the restaurant and he saw Renee laughing about something her mother had said, he'd been awestruck.

She was beautiful, certainly, but no beautiful woman had ever made his jaw drop like that. It was also the first time he'd actually felt nervous when meeting someone. He never felt anxious, even that one time he'd asked out and been summarily dismissed by that supermodel. Aaron had laughed about that one for weeks. Somehow, Renee cut right through what Jessica called his "devil-may-care attitude" and left him feeling awkward and uncertain.

There was something about the way she laughed, the sparkle in her eyes, the way her light red hair fell over her shoulders, the freckles across her nose that made her look wonderfully fresh and happy, the sexy tilt of her chin that seemed to exude self-confidence. Whatever it was, something about her made it hard to think straight.

And even though they'd hardly talked, he had a suspicion that she might just be interested in him, too. When they'd been introduced, a light flush had spread up her neck, and she had let go of his hand just as quickly when they shook for the first time. Like she had felt the same jolt of electricity as he had.

Just the memory of her was enough to make his body jump to attention, and he felt an uncomfortable swelling in his jeans.

Jeremiah took another deep breath, trying to relax his body, and climbed out of the truck. If he could just get through the next hour without doing anything stupid, he would be able to keep his distance from her for the rest of the week and avoid the almost-overwhelming temptation to kiss her.

RENEE STEPPED INTO the airport restroom and went straight to the mirror, looking at the damage done by her flight and trying to put herself back together. She glanced at her skirt and blouse, trying to straighten out the wrinkles, ignoring the tiny voice reminding her that Jeremiah was off-limits.

Of course he was off-limits. She knew that, and he certainly wasn't the reason she'd opted to ditch her comfy travel clothes and instead wear makeup, heels and her black skirt that hugged in the right places—not to mention the silky black underthings. She just thought it would be nice to look her best when she showed up at her sister's house.

The voice laughed at her unconvincing lies.

After taking one last look in the mirror and trying to wish away the dusting of freckles across her nose that made her look like a Girl Scout, she gave herself one more silent pep talk. *Remember, nothing can happen with Jeremiah, and he probably just thinks of you as Jessica's little sister, so seeing him for the first time since Vegas is no big deal. There's definitely no reason for your stomach to feel like this. So stop staring into a mirror like a crazy person and leave this bathroom.*

She didn't budge. Renee swore under her breath at her idiocy and steeled herself for what would assuredly be a very not-sexy week full of helping Jessica and staring at a guy who hardly knew she existed. Then she finally managed to walk out of the bathroom and through the terminal exit doors to baggage claim. She found herself standing in a cavernous room studded with numbered carousels slowly circling luggage.

Her first thought was that she'd never find Jeremiah in this huge area, but that lasted less than four seconds before she spied him standing about twenty yards away, looking at her. Their eyes met, and she froze for a moment like a deer in headlights.

He wasn't as gorgeous as she remembered. He was even more so. Her daydreams hadn't done justice to the way his slightly shaggy, dark hair fell across his forehead or how his shirt clung to his chest. Not to mention his low-slung jeans and what was sure to be underneath. The quivering in her stomach turned into melting, an ache that made her knees feel weak.

Then someone bumped her elbow as they tried to walk around her, and she realized she was blocking the doorway and staring like Meg Ryan in one of her romantic comedies Renee loved to watch. She could feel a blush start low on her cheeks as she imagined how ridiculous she must look to him. How was she ever going to get through an entire drive alone in the car with him without making a complete fool of herself?

Another person knocked against her. She adjusted the bag on her shoulder and started moving toward the sexy cowboy who was waiting for her. As she got closer, Renee smiled and gave a tiny wave, vividly remembering the first time they shook hands. If she was going to get through this, there had to be no touching, that was for sure. If she could keep things casual, everything would be fine and Jessica wouldn't need to kill her for groping someone she hardly knew instead of helping with the wedding.

"Hi, Jeremiah. Thanks for picking me up," she said, hoping she sounded normal.

He smiled back, a little stiffly, making her wonder exactly how inconvenient this errand had been. But then he shrugged and his lips softened. "No problem. I was coming into town anyway. Do you have a bag to pick up?"

She looked up and noticed that the carousel closest to them displayed her flight information and luggage was starting to slide down the chute. She nodded, and after an awkward pause that seemed to stretch between them, she was grateful to see her bag coming her way. Before she could do more than place her hand on it, though, he had it by the handle and was picking it up as if it weighed nothing. She briefly imagined him picking her up with the same strength before stopping herself.

No sexy thoughts, she reminded herself yet again. Jessica freaking out. Jeremiah not interested.

Except something in the way he looked at her made her think that maybe that second one wasn't true.

She tried to shake off the thought as she followed him out of the airport and into the parking structure, where he stopped at a large silver truck that screamed cowboy. It was huge. *Everything's bigger in Texas*, she thought to herself, sneaking a peek at Jeremiah, her mind drifting off into forbidden, jean-clad areas. She couldn't stop herself from smiling.

"What's so funny?" he asked, a good-natured grin on his face as he broke the silence between them.

She blushed for the second time in as many minutes, a bad omen for their drive together. There was definitely no way she would admit where her thoughts had gone, so she thought up something else as quickly as she could. "Nothing. Just the sheer number of trucks. It's all so very...Texas."

He smirked, and her heart skipped a beat. He said, "Most people in the city drive them for that reason. They don't actually get used to haul stuff around."

He settled her suitcase into the truck bed, among a variety of boxes, some plants, a bunch of metal rods and a number of other things Renee couldn't identify.

Before she could reach for the door, he had it open for her and helped her climb in, making her fingers tingle where they touched. She tried to keep her mind on acceptable topics. "You clearly use yours to haul around plenty. What is all that stuff?"

He gave her a crooked grin. "Most of it's for your sister, actually. She had a whole list of things she needed to pick up, and I volunteered since I was coming into town to replace a broken generator."

She looked out the back window and tried to identify the wedding items. "Those metal rods are some kind of arch thing, I'm guessing?" He nodded. "And the plants, of course. And me. She's really putting you to work," Renee finished, laughing.

Jeremiah chuckled and raised an eyebrow. "I'm positive it's nothing compared to what she has in store for you."

Renee laughed again. A little of the awkward tension was gone and she felt lighter than she had since seeing him, but that ache didn't go anywhere. He was even sexier when he was being funny, God help her.

Jeremiah swung the truck out of the parking structure. Renee racked her brain for any safe topics that could keep the silence from settling between them again. When they were quiet, her mind wandered, and she didn't want to spend the entire drive wondering whether or not the bench seat of his vehicle was long enough for them to act out a few of her spicier fantasies.

"So, how far away do you guys live from the airport?"

"You guys?" he repeated with a thick Brooklyn accent. "You're never going to fit in around here with talk like that. We say *y'all* around here."

Renee tried again, this time putting the thickest drawl she could muster into her voice. "Well lookee here, Jeremiah, just how long of a ride do we have in this here fancy horse buggy till we mosey into y'all's neck of the woods?"

He let out a peal of laughter that reverberated through her chest, so loud and genuine that it made her laugh in response. He had an amazing, infectious laugh, and she was swept away in the silliness of the moment. When was the last time she'd joked with a guy? It seemed far too long.

"We all live about sixty miles away," he said, finally getting himself enough under control to answer her question, adding an adorable Texas accent to his words.

An hour alone with him. God help her. Renee looked out the window. The city—if you could call it that—was already shrinking in the distance, leaving them surrounded by a few homes and a lot of open land. "And that's the closest town to you? To get a generator, you need to drive all the way to, um—" she panicked for a moment as she realized she didn't remember the name of the city she had just flown into "—Tyson?" she finished, hoping it was right.

He raised his eyebrow and smiled at her again in the way that made her insides twist. "You mean Tyler?"

She flushed, embarrassed. "Yeah. That."

"There are a couple of small towns that are closer, but Tyler's the biggest nearby. We'll be at Jessica and Aaron's before you know it."

Although that was what she told herself she wanted, the idea was not a pleasant one. She was enjoying talking to Jeremiah, and didn't want it to end *too* quickly. "Was it weird to start calling it 'Jessica and Aaron's' instead of just 'Aaron's place'?"

He thought for a moment, tilting his head. "Not really. They just fit together so well that the moment she moved in, it became their place, you know?"

Renee nodded, but didn't really understand. She looked at the window as they flew past large homes and swaying trees, already well out of the city. The fields in the distance were a wintry brown, showing off a wide expanse of countryside. How did Jessica transplant her whole life to this strange place and settle in so smoothly? Renee felt like a fish out of water looking at the vast nothingness around her.

JEREMIAH TRIED TO keep his eyes on the road, but his gaze was continuously drawn to the woman only a few feet away. He'd been failing miserably at self-control since the moment she walked into baggage claim in that sexy, curve-loving skirt and heels that made him want to drop to his knees and worship her legs. There were a lot of things he'd like to drop to his knees and do to her, in fact.

He focused back on the present, trying to stop those thoughts. They were exactly what he couldn't let himself get caught up in this week if he wanted to survive.

He glanced at her again. Instead of thinking about the way her shirt moved against her breasts as she shifted in her seat, he tried to think of something to say to her.

Her mood had switched from silly to thoughtful in a matter of seconds, and he wasn't sure what he should do. For a guy who'd always felt so confident around women, this was a new one on him.

He grabbed at some new topic of conversation. Anything to keep her talking. "It's nice of you to fly in a week early to help your sister. According to Aaron, she's been fighting off a state of panic for the past week or so, worrying that things won't be ready in time."

Renee nodded, as if this wasn't new information. "She's always been the anxious one. She wouldn't be Jessica if she wasn't worried. Really, though, it should be Cindy here. She's always been the enthusiastic, creative one. I'm not sure how I'm going to be able to help much, but with the pregnancy and all, Cindy couldn't take that much time off from work."

"If Jessica's the anxious one and Cindy's the enthusiastic one, what are you?" He wasn't sure if he was prying, but he just had to know more about her.

She paused, thinking. "I guess I'm the focused, driven one."

Jeremiah tried to read between the lines. "Is that code for 'workaholic?'"

Renee gave him a small smile. "Pretty much."

"And what else are you?"

She shrugged. "I don't know. I think that's about it."

He could think of some other adjectives that described her, but didn't say them out loud. He wasn't sure if she even realized she was the funny one, the sexy one, the dear-God-I-wish-she-was-in-my-arms-right-now one.

He tried to think of something else to talk about. Normally he'd be fine with silence, but silence around her made him want to say and do things that were all on the "terrible ideas" list. At least when they were talking, he could focus on their conversation instead of on the way her hair fell across her shoulders and that one darker freckle just below her left ear.

Lucky for him, she seemed just as willing to keep up continuous chatter as he was, and the rest of the drive passed quickly while she described her favorite things about New York, asked questions about her sister's life in Texas and told him about her job.

"It's not a sure thing yet, but the lead designer spot would be amazing. I've been working toward that exact position since high school. It's my dream job."

He glanced at her out of the side of his eye, even though her face was already indelibly printed in his mind. She couldn't possibly be older than twenty-eight. "You've managed to land your dream job before turning thirty? Is that some kind of a record?"

Renee smiled and her eyes lit up, changing her face from beautiful to stunning. "I'm younger than a lot of people on my team, but I have just as much experience as pretty much anyone there if you look at the work I've done. I usually pick up a few extra pages each issue, and my work hardly ever needs to be retouched. I don't think my age will matter."

"I guess you were right about being the workaholic one."

"That was your word," she pointed out. "I said I was the focused one."

Jeremiah was impressed, but something about her dedication to her job sent up an alarm. "How do you manage to do all that and still have fun? Doesn't it make it hard to relax, take vacations, date?"

Jessica had mentioned at one point that Renee was single—Jeremiah was sure she had no idea how that offhand comment had affected him—and he'd been perplexed as to why. Now he was beginning to suspect the reason.

"I don't really have the time for that kind of stuff. My job is too important to me and I wouldn't want to screw that up because of those types of distractions."

Renee's shrug seemed casual, but her voice sounded very serious to him. Jeremiah wondered if she was sending him a message between the lines. If she was, he got it loud and clear.

Even though he'd known from the start that there would be no dating this woman, here was yet another example of why he needed to let go of all the little fantasies and quit mooning over her.

For a guy who was normally so great at looking on the bright side of things, he couldn't seem to find the silver lining for this one.

Relief swept through him as he drove up to Jessica and Aaron's house. He'd made it through the entire drive without saying or doing anything inappropriate, and now he could try to keep his distance and avoid being alone with her for the rest of her visit. Once she went back to New York, it would probably be years before he saw her again.

He didn't enjoy that thought.

He parked on the side of the large yellow ranch house, angling the truck so it would be easy to empty the wedding contents from the back. After turning off the engine, he shifted to look at Renee, who had turned her body toward him, as if she wanted to say something.

"Thanks for the ride, Jeremiah," she said, and he looked into her eyes deeply for the first time since they had left the airport.

It was no problem.

Anything for Jessica's sister.

That's what you do for friends.

All of the correct responses died in his throat. There was only one way he wanted to answer her, and before he knew what he was doing, he leaned across the small distance between them and pressed his lips to hers, his hand grazing across the soft skin of her cheek.

It took him less than a second to realize how awful that decision was, but then she pressed back into him, parting her lips and tilting her head, her urgency matching his. Any self-control he could have used to pull away dissipated when her tongue slid against his, sending tendrils of heat through his entire body.

His hand slid from her cheek down her neck, slowly inching lower. Before he could fall deeper into the kiss or his hand could move past her collarbone, though, she leaned back, separating from him. Her breathing was heavy and her eyes wide, and he realized what had just happened. He rubbed his hand across his face and tore his eyes away from her, checking to be sure Jessica was nowhere in sight. Dear God, he'd kissed her. How could he have been so stupid?

Still, he couldn't help but feel excitement course through him. She had kissed him, too. He looked at her again. She was shaking her head, her eyes closed, her hands covering her face.

"I'm so sorry—" he began.

"That was so bad," she moaned, cutting him off.

He grimaced. "The kiss was bad?" he asked, unable to help himself.

She shook her head even more furiously. "The kiss was too good. That's what makes it so bad."

Jeremiah knew he should feel awful, but he was happier than he'd been in a very long time. Just to be sure, he asked, "So you liked the kiss?"

She looked at him through her fingers. "That's not helping. There's no way we can do that again. Jessica will flip if she finds out. She doesn't take unexpected new information well, and this is her *wedding* week. A curveball like that might send her into seizures."

Jeremiah wasn't sure if Renee was talking to him or herself, but her arguments seemed much less convincing than they might have been a few minutes before. There seemed to be one pretty glaring way around the issue, after all. "I'm not going to tell her about it. Are you?"

"No way," Renee responded immediately.

"So..." he said slowly, picking his words with care, "if neither of us tells her, and she doesn't see us, is there any reason why we can't do it again?"

3

Renee was about to roll her eyes at Jeremiah and explain exactly why they could never do anything like that again, but something stopped her before she could. Her libido spoke up with full force, demanding why exactly that was such a terrible idea.

She'd been thinking about this guy for weeks, and here he was offering her a chance to live out a few of those fantasies that had been running through her mind. It wasn't like she'd have another chance this good again.

And the look on his face wasn't helping her make any prudent decisions, either. The hope in his eyes combined with a smile that promised so much more. How could she let this opportunity go by?

Renee took a deep breath and looked out the front windshield in order to keep herself from leaning toward Jeremiah again. She tried to focus some of her attention on the view, but the trees and mountains spread before her were overshadowed by the sexy cowboy sitting inches away. "Okay," she answered, and out of the corner of her eye she saw his smile widen into a full grin. She had to force herself not to smile back. "But," she continued, "there have to be ground rules. Number one—Jessica and Aaron absolutely can*not* find out about this. Jessica would turn it into such a big deal, and even though Aaron's your best friend, he might tell Jessica. And number two—once I go home, we're done. This is just a casual thing. Just sex."

She continued looking out the windshield, waiting for a response, but was met with silence. It was only then that she realized he'd never said anything about them having sex. They'd had one two-second kiss and she had already good as told him that she was ready to jump into bed with him at a moment's notice. What kind of woman did that make her?

The kind of woman that hadn't gotten laid in a long time and had spent way too much time thinking about getting laid by this particular guy. But had she gone too far too quickly?

She looked over at him, hoping for some kind of positive response. Jeremiah was looking at her, that half smile still on his face.

JEREMIAH STARED AT RENEE, surprised. She couldn't get much more straightforward than that. Just sex? He had given up the casual-sex thing months ago, and was serious about finding something more than that. Did he really want a secret one-week fling? To risk hurting his best friend's fiancée for something that would be over in just a few days?

Then she looked at him, her green eyes silently questioning, and reminded himself that Jessica wouldn't find out, and therefore couldn't be hurt. He knew it was a weak argument, but really, there was only one answer he could possibly give this beautiful woman beside him.

He leaned forward again, pulling her into another kiss, this one slow and deep, full of the promise of more to come.

She responded immediately, falling into the kiss, but he pulled away after just a few moments. The indignant expression on her face made him want to laugh. The way her erect nipples showed through her shirt made him want to tear her clothes off. He took a breath. "Rule number one, remember? It'll probably be pretty hard to keep this thing a secret if Jessica finds us making out in front of her house."

Renee's eyes grew wide and she turned to look out the back window, searching for her sister, worry evident on her face. This time he couldn't stop the laughter.

Once she had carefully scanned for any sign of Jessica, she looked back at him and smiled. "Right, so maybe this isn't the most discreet location."

He knew they only had a few more seconds of privacy together, and he didn't want to separate without planning something. He needed to have another opportunity to kiss her in the near future, or it would drive him crazy. "When can we meet?"

She shrugged. "I don't know what Jessica has planned for me. I might be able to get away at some point tonight, but won't you need to go home?"

Jeremiah smiled. "I think I can manage to stick around here for the evening."

She looked like she was about to say something else, but before she could, a door somewhere nearby closed loudly and two voices started moving toward them. Jeremiah tried not to look too disappointed. "That'll be Jessica and Aaron," he said, opening his door and tearing his eyes away from the beauty next to him.

He climbed out of the truck cab just as Aaron and his tall, leggy fiancée walked around the corner of the house. Before Jeremiah could walk around the truck to help Renee down, she was clambering out herself and moving with quick footsteps to hug her sister.

Jeremiah watched, comparing the two women. At first glance, they looked very different: Jessica was tall, with long auburn hair and lightly tanned skin. Renee looked almost petite next to her, though she couldn't be under five foot six, with strawberry blonde locks barely grazing her shoulders and freckles dotting her pale cheeks and nose.

There were plenty of similarities when looked at more closely, though. They had the same shape of face, and something about the way they stood made it clear they were related.

He watched them embrace, their wide smiles nearly identical. He kept looking at Renee, studying the way she held herself, the tilt of her head, and thinking about what he might expect when they managed to find themselves alone together. Would she be as straightforward as her talk and her kisses implied? If so, he was in for one hell of a week.

He relived the kiss in his mind, feeling the sensations again as her tongue slid across his teeth. His heart revved back up to sprinting speed just thinking about it.

"Hey man, thanks for grabbing all that stuff and picking up Renee and everything," Aaron said, startling Jeremiah out of his reverie. While he'd been absorbed in every movement Renee made, he had completely failed to notice that his friend had come up beside him.

Jeremiah looked at Aaron and tried to sound casual, as if he hadn't been mentally undressing his buddy's sister-in-law. "No problem."

"Everything okay?" Aaron asked, his forehead creasing as he lifted an eyebrow. "You seem a little distracted or something."

Jeremiah wanted to smack himself. It hadn't even been two minutes and Aaron could already tell something was up. How was he going to manage to keep this thing quiet? It didn't help that he was a horrible liar. He just had to act normal, that's all. Jeremiah shrugged and replied, "I'm fine," then waited to see if he had pulled it off.

Aaron looked at his friend for another moment, then moved toward the bed of Jeremiah's truck. "Let's get this stuff unloaded," he said.

Glad to be out of the spotlight, Jeremiah immediately went to work.

JESSICA HUGGED HER AGAIN. "It's great to see you! How was your flight? And the drive in? I hope it was okay that Jeremiah picked you up."

More than okay, thought Renee as she glanced at Jeremiah, who was standing with Aaron. Just the sight of him made her heart beat loud in her chest, and she hoped she hadn't started blushing. She suddenly felt warm despite the cool February weather.

"Everything's been great. I'm ready to be put to work. Should we start unloading the truck?"

Before she could even turn to make good on the offer, though, Aaron and Jeremiah were tackling the job. Jeremiah climbed into his silver monolith of a vehicle, and Aaron shook his head at the two women. "We'll take care of this. You ladies go catch up."

Jessica ran over to her fiancé and gave him a kiss, which seemed to Renee as if it was going to turn into much more when Aaron looped his arm around Jessica's waist and lifted her up, pressing her body against his. Renee looked at Jeremiah again, and found him looking back at her and smiling. She wasn't sure if it was because of his friend's antics or because he was thinking of what he would do to her when he got the chance to get an arm around her. The latter was probably wishful thinking and she was definitely projecting some of her own thoughts on him.

But a girl could hope.

Then Jessica was back, a little breathless. She grabbed Renee's hand and started steering her toward the front of the house.

"Are you sure we shouldn't help?" Renee asked, partly because her New York sensibilities rankled a bit at the idea of letting the guys do all the work and partly because she wanted to watch Jeremiah using those very sexy muscles she could see straining beneath his shirt.

She didn't let herself think about how much weight each reason held in her mind.

Jessica shrugged. "Nah. It's a bit of a battle trying to get these Texas boys to stop doing stuff for us. They're very gentlemanly. There are definitely worse problems to have. Anyway, I want to show you around and hear how things are going, so we can let them win this one."

If Texas is a state where "letting the guys win" means sitting back while they unload a full truck, maybe it isn't such a bad place after all.

She had without doubt warmed up to Texas over the past ten minutes. And if she kept thinking about Jeremiah's lips against hers, it would soon become one of her favorite places.

Before Jessica could pull her around the corner, Renee took one look at Jeremiah. He stood in the back of his truck, his body all muscle and hard lines, which made the perpetual smile crinkling his lips and eyes that much more breathtaking.

JEREMIAH WATCHED RENEE disappear around the corner of the house. Just before she was out of sight, she turned and gave him a smile. Not the sweet smile he'd seen her use on her sister, or the tentative one he'd seen when he first picked her up from the airport. This smile held a promise that made his pulse pound in his ears. It was only for a moment, but it was enough.

He had to figure out how to get her alone as soon as possible, or he might internally combust from all the heat flowing through his veins.

He would have kept staring at the place where he'd

last seen her, picturing all the things that smile hinted at, but Aaron interrupted his train of thought.

"You're staying for dinner, right?"

You couldn't drag me away. Aloud, though, all he said was, "Yeah, if that's okay."

Aaron nodded distractedly as he started pulling at the assorted bars and wires which would eventually become a wedding arch. Jeremiah moved to help him. As they pulled out each wedding-related item, Jeremiah said, "It looks like there's still quite a bit to do before the ceremony next weekend. Will everything be done in time?"

He really wanted to ask if Renee would have any free time at all or if Jessica would keep her so busy that he would almost never see her, but he couldn't think of a way to say it that didn't sound too much like he was asking when he'd be able to bang Aaron's sister-in-law.

"It should be pretty simple, actually, but Jessica wants to double-check everything, so that'll take some time."

"She's really putting in the effort to make sure nothing unexpected happens, huh?"

Jeremiah didn't know why he would ask that. Maybe he was trying to remind himself exactly why he had to keep his hands off Renee. In public, at least.

Aaron smiled what Jeremiah called his "Jessica smile." It was full of love, pure and simple. "Jessica wants everything to be as planned as possible, and she's willing to do everything she can to make that happen."

Jeremiah had no idea why that made Aaron smile, but he was glad his friend was so happy. Ever since

Aaron had met Jessica in Las Vegas two years ago, he'd been happier than Jeremiah had ever seen him.

Being in love definitely didn't seem that bad.

RENEE SAT AT the small circular kitchen table, trying not to fidget with her cup of tea. What was taking Jeremiah and Aaron so long?

After Jessica had taken Renee on a quick tour of the large, beautiful home she shared with Aaron, complete with white lace curtains like something out of a movie, they had settled into the kitchen so Jessica could keep an eye on dinner while they went over her notebook of wedding details to complete that week.

If Renee hadn't been so focused on finding some time to get Jeremiah to herself, she would've probably had trouble not rolling her eyes at her sister's binder full of lists, receipts and diagrams. It was detailed to the point of seeming neurotic.

Finally, after Jessica was nearly through all the pages regarding flowers, the back door opened and Aaron walked in, followed by Jeremiah. Aaron went over to the stove to check on something bubbling in a pot, while Jeremiah leaned against the counter near the back door they had just entered.

Jessica stopped her monologue and joined Aaron in the inspection of the meal, and Renee took advantage of the moment free from her sister's view to take in all the glory of the man from her fantasies as he moved toward her. She stared at his jean-clad legs and slowly moved her eyes up his body, lingering on a few choice places. God, he was gorgeous. It made her breath catch in her throat.

When she finally reached his face, he was looking right at her, a sexy smile on his lips, as if he knew exactly what she'd been doing. His eyebrows were raised in question, and she gave him her final assessment with a smile of her own and the tiniest of nods. She very much approved of what she saw.

At the end of their silent conversation, Jeremiah turned to the two talking at the stove. He said, "I'll take Renee's suitcase upstairs and get her set up in a guest room."

Renee jumped up from the table, nearly knocking over her tea, in her eagerness to follow him out of the room. After he'd gotten the nod from the couple and started to make his way toward the stairs with her suitcase, though, she hesitated for a moment. Was this really such a good idea? Flirting and some quick kisses in his truck were one thing, but was she really going to go through with this idea? The whole clandestine affair thing was so not like her.

But then Jeremiah turned and crooked a half smile and her insides melted, and she knew she wouldn't give up this opportunity for anything. She scurried after him up the stairs, nearly bowling into him on the landing, where he'd stopped to wait for her.

As soon as she was near enough, he wrapped an arm around her waist and pulled her in close, pressing her body against his. She gasped at the heat and strength she could feel where her breasts and stomach touched him. Her nipples budded at the contact.

The force of her reaction to him made her nervous for a moment, but then he was kissing her and her ability to think evaporated.

As soon as his mouth was against hers, every notion of stopping fell away at once, and she leaned even closer into his heat. In the truck, the first kiss had been quick and impulsive; the second short, slow and full of promise. This one, however, could only be described as passionate. Very very passionate.

So passionate she was vaguely surprised her clothes didn't disintegrate on contact.

Jeremiah's tongue plunged into her mouth, taking everything he could, but giving so much in the process. Time slowed as every ounce of her focused on the physical sensations: the feel of his mouth against hers, the tingling of her fingers, the warm heat that had pooled low in her belly, making her push against his body even harder.

And what she felt there, hot and hard against her, only turned her on more.

JEREMIAH HATED TO pull away from Renee's kiss yet again, but he managed to force himself to break away, though he kept his arm around her waist. When she tried to lean back in, he chuckled. She was deliciously disheveled, and he wanted both to tuck her hair behind her ear and to mess it up even more. He was able to keep himself in check, though. "We should probably move to someplace a little more…private…than here."

Renee looked down the stairs, as if she expected to see Jessica looking up and glaring at them. "Right," she said once she seemed sure that they were still alone. Her voice was low and she sounded out of breath, which sent even more blood pumping straight to his already-painful erection. "Which room is mine?" she asked, looking at the doors on both sides of the hallway.

Jeremiah gestured with his chin to the door on the left, keeping his eyes on her lips, only just able to keep himself from kissing her again. She broke away and turned to open the door. He reluctantly let her withdraw from his embrace. It surprised him how much he hated to have her leave his side, even if it was only for the moment it took to get inside the room.

He lifted her suitcase and followed her into the room, hoping he hadn't ruined the moment enough that he'd just be setting down the luggage and walking back downstairs, but he didn't have to wait long to be satisfied on that count.

He walked into the room and only had enough time to notice that Renee hadn't turned on the overhead light, leaving the room in only the dim sunlight filtering through the window, before the door was closing behind him. He turned around just as the door clicked shut and Renee rushed back into his arms, picking up right where they'd left off.

Every curve of her was touching him, driving him wild. He pressed against her until she was backed up against the door, slipping one hand under her shirt. She moaned deep in the back of her throat as his hand slid up from her waist to her breast, and he echoed the sound as his fingers found her nipple, hard and erect.

He teased the peaked tip as he moved his mouth to

her earlobe, eliciting another moan from her, and his unoccupied hand moved down to her thigh. Jeremiah knew they didn't have much time, but he planned to take full advantage of this moment. The skirt she was wearing had ridden up dangerously high, leaving so much of her shapely legs exposed for his viewing pleasure. He drank in the sight as he pulled the skirt even higher, wishing the room was brighter so he could see Renee in all her glory.

When his fingers slid past her lacy panties to her folds, she gasped, and his entire body tensed as he felt her wet heat. He put his mouth to the place on her neck where her heartbeat throbbed as he stroked her with his fingers, dipping first one inside her, then two, and continuing to rub at her mound until she was holding on to him tightly, her head pressed back against the door, her eyes closed.

RENEE COULD BARELY stand as Jeremiah continued stroking her core, kissing along her throat and teasing her breast. He was playing her like a violin and damn if he wasn't good at it. The growing tension low in her belly built until she couldn't resist the wave as it crashed over her. She came hard, her entire body shivering with it as it ran through her.

She opened her eyes and saw Jeremiah smiling at her, his eyes smoldering with barely controlled need. And how she wanted to fill that need.

Renee reached down to the button of his jeans, anticipation boiling inside her. Just as she pulled down the zipper and moved to expose what, from the feel of it against the fabric, was a huge erection however, Jessica's voice floated in from downstairs.

"Dinner's ready! Time to eat!"

Damn. Renee stopped what she was doing and looked at Jeremiah. His expression was so pained that it made her laugh.

"Really? This is funny?" he asked, a smile crossing his own lips.

Renee leaned her head forward, letting it rest against Jeremiah's chest as she tried to take a few breaths to calm herself down. But when she breathed in his scent, a mixture of some cologne that made her think of the outdoors and his own masculine smell, she had to lean back again. She wasn't ready to go be around her sister and talk wedding so soon after that spectacular orgasm.

As if Jeremiah knew what she was thinking, he took a deep breath of his own. "I'll head down first," he said. "I can tell them you're getting settled in your room and washing up."

He sent one last smile her way as she moved away from the door, and then he was gone.

One thing she could say for him: Jeremiah was a good sport.

4

RENEE TOOK A shuddering breath and moved away from the door Jeremiah had just closed behind him, flicking the light on as she went. The house was large and had several guest rooms, each a different color. She suspected this was Jessica's doing—it seemed very much like her sister to tell someone that they were staying in "the blue room," and then give them a set of towels that matched.

Renee was in the green room, the mint-colored walls bright and friendly in the light thrown from the bedside lamp. Green vines crisscrossed the white background of the bedspread, and even the white chest of drawers had green accents. It was all so sweet and pretty that she had to smile.

She opened her suitcase on the floor and grabbed out a pair of pants and some fresh underwear, sliding out of the clothes that were suggestively mussed from her interaction with Jeremiah and putting on the new outfit, trying to flatten her hair as she did so. After a glance in the mirror and a swipe at her smeared makeup, she readied herself to go back downstairs.

She took one last calming breath, opened the door and made her way to where the rest of the group sat. When she stepped into the kitchen, she found quite the happy scene: Aaron's arm around the back of Jessica's chair, her body leaning into his and both of them laughing at something Jeremiah must have just said. He looked a little embarrassed, but was laughing, too. Everyone seemed comfortable and content, almost like a little family. How did she fit in here?

Her good mood sank a little as she realized that she didn't. They were all Texas, and she was New York.

But then Jeremiah looked in her direction and his eyes lit up at the sight of her, and she was able to push those thoughts aside. She didn't need to belong here. She would have a great week, fulfill a few fantasies, and then go back to New York to her dream job.

That was better than belonging in this little group, she told herself.

By the time she'd gone through these thoughts and felt reassured that her life was already everything she could want, really, Jessica had spotted her. She gestured at the full plate and empty seat clearly meant for her. "Come and get some food. I'm sure you haven't had a decent home-cooked meal since…when was the last time you ate at Mom's?"

Renee thought for a second as she sat down. "Almost two weeks ago."

"What have you been living on since then?"

Renee didn't want to answer, especially with Jeremiah watching her, that perpetual grin on his face, as if he was enjoying the interaction. "This and that," she answered vaguely.

Jessica raised her eyebrows. "Sandwiches from the deli down the street and leftover pizza?"

"Veggie pizza," Renee added, knowing that it didn't make it sound any better. "I'm busy. And I don't know how to cook. This looks amazing," she said in an attempt to change the subject from her terrible eating habits.

Jessica smiled, clearly proud of herself. "It's just an easy chicken recipe. Now get to eating," she said, pointing at the plate.

Renee took a bite, reveling in the taste of fresh vegetables and roasted chicken. She really needed to eat real food more often, but after working all day, she was too exhausted to do more than grab something on the way to her apartment or toss old pizza in the microwave. Another thing to push from her mind. This was not the week to examine her faults.

"What were you laughing about when I came in?" she asked, trying to get the conversation going on another topic.

Aaron smiled at her. "Jeremiah was telling Jessica about the time he was hitting on our waitress at a diner in Tyler."

Renee forced herself to smile, trying to tell herself that it was good to remember that Jeremiah wasn't a settle-down kind of guy. According to the stories Jessica had told her, in fact, he was more of a hit-on-any-female-with-a-pulse kind of guy.

And that was very good, because there was no way she'd be falling for him. Fantasy sex only.

"TELL HER WHAT HAPPENED," Aaron prompted, hitting Jeremiah lightly on the shoulder.

Jeremiah looked down at his plate, his blood pumping hard. Aaron had brought it up in the first place, and now he had to tell Renee about hitting on other women. Great.

He wanted to punch Aaron "playfully" on the arm, at least hard enough to leave a bruise, but he didn't want to raise any eyebrows. There was no way he'd forget Renee's number one rule and ruin the possibility of an amazing week.

"It was *years* ago," he clarified, hoping Renee understood that he wasn't that guy anymore.

Aaron leaned in toward Renee, clearly missing Jeremiah's discomfort. "We sat down to get some lunch, and Jeremiah just *has* to hit on the really hot waitress. Because he's Jeremiah and isn't afraid to get turned down by anyone."

Jeremiah forced himself not to glare at his friend. He had to keep it casual, no matter how much he wanted to kill the guy. *If he tries to tell the story about the supermodel,* he thought, *I'll tackle him right here at the table.*

Aaron continued the story, completely oblivious. "He must have asked her out or made sexual innuendos one too many times, because, you know those 'We reserve the right to refuse service' signs? Yeah, I had to drive home hungry all because Jeremiah thought he might be able to get laid in the walk-in freezer or something."

Aaron laughed again at the story. Jeremiah looked over to Renee to see her reaction. She was smiling and nodding, but he didn't like the look in her eyes. Stupid Aaron.

After a silence that felt way too long to Jeremiah, Aaron started talking again. "Hey Jeremiah, tell Renee what happened with the—"

If he says supermodel I'm going to destroy him, Jeremiah thought, holding his fork in a death grip.

"—generator," Aaron finished, to Jeremiah's immense relief.

That was another embarrassing story, but at least it didn't make him look like an asshole.

Jeremiah launched into the story before Aaron could say anything else. "Okay, so my generator was out of gas, right? Luckily, I have a few gas cans sitting around and poured some gas into it. Or at least what I thought was gas…"

RENEE WATCHED JEREMIAH go through the whole story, laughing aloud as he gestured wildly to show exactly how thick the smoke was as it billowed from the ruined piece of machinery.

For the most part, though, her attention wasn't on his epic tale. It was on the width of his shoulders, the way his hair fell across his forehead, the mischievous glint in his eyes, the strength of his arms.

God, she wanted him. Just looking at him from across the table made her squirm in her seat. And judging by the performance upstairs, it was going to be amazing once they managed to get more than five minutes alone together.

She'd never felt so impatient in her life.

After dinner, Jessica turned to Renee and said, "Well, tomorrow we'll start with the wedding stuff, but tonight I want to catch up, if you aren't completely exhausted."

Renee looked at her sister's smile and tried to smile back, but it wasn't easy. She realized that none of the scenarios running through her mind, most of which involved Jeremiah tearing pieces of clothing from her body, was going to happen tonight. There was just no way to get Jeremiah alone without letting Jessica in on the situation, which absolutely wasn't going to happen. Stupid rule number one.

Renee could see that Jeremiah realized it, too, and he didn't look too happy about it.

Dinner flew by. Renee tried not to look at Jeremiah, but constantly caught herself glancing over to where he sat. He seemed all casual confidence, and the ease he exuded amazed her. How could he be so relaxed after that little episode upstairs?

After dinner was done and the talk had lulled, though, his demeanor changed. Almost as if he should leave, but he didn't want to. She didn't want him to leave, either, but there was nothing to be done.

Finally, Jessica pulled the notebook out again and Jeremiah said his goodbyes. His eyes lingered on Renee for an extra second before he turned away. She watched as he walked out the door.

She cursed to herself. That was one opportunity gone.

Jessica had started talking to her, but she'd missed

it. All Renee could think about was how she couldn't wait until some unknown time to kiss him again. And what if she never got the chance?

She could hardly bear the thought. She was too close to let this lie.

"I think I left my phone in Jeremiah's truck," she blurted out, then rushed to the door without waiting for her sister to comment.

She imagined getting to his truck just before he pulled away and giving him one hell of a sensuous kiss that would leave him thinking of her all night.

Renee was off the porch and rounding the corner of the house in a blink, only to see Jeremiah just a couple feet away, walking toward her and directly in her path. She couldn't stop herself in time and ran into him at full speed with a very unsexy "Oof."

Slamming into his chest was like hitting a brick wall, and she bounced off and fell to the ground, the wind knocked out of her. As she sat in the dirt, a little cloud of dust settling around her, she was glad it was dim enough that he couldn't see how red her cheeks were.

Jeremiah knelt close. "Are you all right?" he asked, trying to look her over for damage.

Even through her embarrassment, she couldn't help but feel aroused. His hand, which was resting casually on her thigh, took her attention away from how silly she must look sprawled on the ground.

She stood, brushing dirt off herself. "I don't know which is bruised more—my butt or my ego," she murmured, half to herself.

He stopped his ministrations and cocked his head

to one side. "That sounds familiar. Is that a quote from a movie?"

She was stunned he recognized it. "It's from *It Takes Two*. Why do you know an obscure quote from a decades-old movie made for little girls?"

Jeremiah laughed. "I have a little sister. She loved those movies. Haven't thought about them in years."

There was a quiet moment. Then, "What were you doing running around the house?" he asked, the smile on his face indicating that he had a pretty good guess as to the answer.

Renee suddenly felt shy. It was one thing to run up and kiss someone, and another thing entirely to explain that plan while brushing dirt off your ass.

His smile widened as the silence grew, and before she could figure out a way to explain without making herself sound like a dork, he leaned in close and kissed her. His lips and tongue drove any thoughts of embarrassment from her mind. In fact, they drove out pretty much everything that wasn't X-rated.

And then, yet again, the kiss was ended far too soon. Renee briefly considered hopping into Jeremiah's truck and going with him to his place before coming to her senses. She cursed Jessica under her breath.

Jeremiah stepped back, creating enough distance between them that she was able to get herself under control. Mostly.

"I better get going," he said, but he made no move to turn around and walk to his truck.

"Are you going to be around tomorrow?"

She had to ask. It would kill her to spend the next

twenty-four hours wondering when they could continue where they had left off upstairs. It made her knees wobbly just thinking about it.

He grinned. "Can't get enough of me, huh?"

She leaned in, pressing her body against every inch of his. "From that bulge in your pants, I don't think you've had enough, either."

She backed up, watching the pain of separation cross his face and feeling exactly the same. Her little tease was just as bad for her, and she almost regretted having made the move in the first place.

He let out a deep breath. "I haven't had anywhere near enough. I'll find a reason to be here tomorrow."

The thought sent a thrill through her.

Reluctantly, they went their separate ways. Renee heard the door of his truck close behind her as she entered the house, wishing she was spread out on the bench seat of that truck.

"Did you find it?"

Renee almost asked what Jessica was talking about before her brain caught up, remembering her excuse for running out there in the first place. "Oh. No. It must be in my bag somewhere," she replied, hoping she wasn't blushing.

Jessica didn't seem to see anything off about her behavior, which was a relief. Before Renee knew it, she was settled on the couch, tea in hand, her sister relaxing next to her. "We'll be talking wedding all week, I'm sure, but for right now I really want to hear what's happening back in New York."

Renee raised an eyebrow. "We talk every week. How much do you think you're missing?"

"Lots!" Jessica exclaimed. "I want face-to-face communication. So start talking."

"Actually, I do have some news."

Jessica leaned forward. "Guy news?"

Renee had to laugh. "No, work news."

Jessica deflated a little. "All you ever have is work news. You work too much. When was the last time you went out with a guy?"

Renee thought for a moment. Not counting those kisses with Jeremiah, it had been... Well, longer than she'd like to admit.

Before she could formulate an answer, Jessica shook her head and said, "I thought so. What's your work news?"

Renee told her sister about the meeting with Patty. By the time she finished, Jessica's eyes were wide. "That's a lot of responsibility. I'm so happy for you, but does this mean you'll be working more than you already do?"

Jessica, always the worrier. Renee shrugged. "Patty always managed to keep things in balance. I'm sure I'll be fine."

She didn't want to admit to her sister that she was prepared to throw herself into this job with everything she had. If it meant a few more hours at the office, what did it matter? What else did she have to do?

The evening passed quickly, the two sisters swapping stories from their lives. Renee tried to stay focused on the moment, but her mind kept wandering to its two favorite subjects: work and Jeremiah.

If she wasn't designing the perfect layout for the magazine's next issue, she was imagining Jeremiah's hands running all over her.

After the third time she caught herself with no idea what Jessica had been saying, Renee smiled apologetically at her sister. "I'm sorry, but I'm exhausted."

Jessica jumped up, shaking her head. "Of course you are. I don't know what I was thinking. We can talk more tomorrow."

With that, she disappeared down a hallway and came back with fluffy yellow towels in her arms. "Here are some towels in case you want to rinse off before going to bed."

Renee was amused. "And I was betting the towels would be green to match my room. I guess I was wrong on that one."

Jessica looked appalled. "You put your things in the green room? You're supposed to be in the yellow room across the hall."

Renee tried not to laugh. The towels were color-coordinated with each room. The woman was insane. Aloud, she just said, "It's fine, I can move. I'm sure you went to a lot of trouble to get towels that matched the rooms exactly. I can't go ruining that."

Jessica seemed relieved. "Thanks. I didn't buy towels that matched each room, though. Aaron's mom did that."

Before Renee could comment on how neurotic that was, Jessica sighed and looked down at the towels. "Such a good organizer. I wish I could have met her. We would have gotten along so well."

Renee shut her mouth and said nothing. Jessica

turned and began leading her to the stairs. Over her shoulder, she said, "I don't know why I didn't think to tell Jeremiah to put you in the yellow room. Since that's usually his room, he would never have known that you needed to take it over for this week, but we just don't have space to spare with everyone coming in for the wedding."

Renee stumbled, but managed to get her feet back under her. She was going to be staying in the guest room Jeremiah had slept in. With the sheets he slept in and the towels he used if he ever took a shower here.

She pictured him, slick with water, wearing only one of the canary yellow towels, somehow managing to make the color incredibly sensual.

Oh Lordy. She needed help.

Be casual, she reminded herself. "Jeremiah has his own room here?"

Jessica nodded without turning around. "We have more room than we need, and it means he can spend the evening over here drinking and hanging out without worrying about how to get home. We like having him around. He's a great guy."

Renee didn't need to be told that. He was a lot of adjectives. *Sexy, fun, incredibly attractive. Great* was certainly on the list.

After Jessica helped Renee move her luggage into the correct room, Jessica turned to her sister and threw her arms around her in a tight hug. "I'm really glad you're here, Renee. I know that you don't like to take time off work. I just want my wedding to go smoothly, with no surprises, and I don't think I could do it without your help."

Renee thought of Jeremiah and felt guilty. If she was going to keep Jessica from finding out, they would need to be more discreet than they had been so far. She didn't want to be the reason Jessica was unhappy so close to the wedding.

Really, it would be better if she just broke off the thing with him entirely. It's not like she had time in her life for a guy anyway, and a one-week fling wasn't like her. Maybe it would be best to stop now before things became even more complicated than they already were.

Even as she considered backing out, she dismissed it. There was something there with Jeremiah that she couldn't let pass by. Even if it was only for a week.

She hugged her sister back, keeping all her thoughts to herself, and silently promised to be a good sister and help her have exactly the wedding she wanted.

No surprises.

5

JEREMIAH TOSSED AND turned all night, thinking of Renee. The way her hair fell in her face when she leaned forward, the way the corner of her lips turned up when she said something clever, the way she squeezed her eyes shut as she came.

Especially that last one.

Why couldn't she be a girl he'd just met at random? Why did it have to be Jessica's little sister? If she'd been anybody else, he would have asked her out to dinner. And breakfast. Lots of them.

Not that he was entirely sure she would even agree to dinner. From the little she'd told him about her life, it seemed likely she would have told him she was too busy with work to date.

And that bothered him even more than needing to keep the whole thing a secret. After all, it was only a secret because she wanted nothing but a week of sex. If this was more, wouldn't she be okay with telling Jessica?

She didn't want more, though.

But what did he want? He wasn't sure, but it didn't seem like eight days of Renee would be enough.

He stretched out in his very empty bed, reminding himself that he would just need to go with it. Anything to get to see her eyes squeezed shut like that again.

The next morning, Jeremiah watched the clock, forcing himself to wait. After what seemed like an eternity, it was past nine and he could text without making Aaron suspicious.

He double-checked the message he'd written to be sure it gave nothing away before sending it. His phone made a *woosh* sound as the text rushed off to Aaron's phone.

He responded two long minutes later: We could definitely use some help. Jessica wants to organize the stuff for the ceremony today. Come over whenever.

Jeremiah grinned at his phone. He was sure he could find a way to pull Renee aside for a few minutes without anyone noticing, and he was going to take advantage of any possible chance they had.

RENEE DUG INTO her plate of eggs, bacon and hash browns, savoring the taste of another meal not purchased from a stand or heated up in the microwave. She hadn't felt this good in a long time. Fresh food and a great night's sleep did wonders. Even though she was still feeling antsy, wondering when she would see Jeremiah next, the orgasm he'd given her the evening before was still working its magic, and she had slept hard and deep almost as soon as her head had hit the pillow.

Not before she had inhaled the faint scent of Jeremiah, though. It seemed to be embedded in the pillows in her room. The smell had engulfed her as she drifted off, and greeted her this morning when she awoke. If only she could get his scent wrapped around her while still attached to his body.

She wanted to ask Aaron when his friend would be around, but there was no way she could think of to say it casually, so she forced herself to push that to the back of her mind and give her attention to the delicious meal in front of her.

"Aaron, this is amazing," she called over to her almost-brother-in-law, who waved off her compliment with a smile and went back to his cooking.

He was standing next to the stove in a ridiculous apron. It was a sickly pink with frills and pictures of baking utensils and hundreds of cats, of all things. Renee turned to her sister, who was sitting next to her inhaling her own plate. "Why does Aaron have an apron like that?" she asked, needing to know the story behind the awful accessory.

Jessica laughed and shook her head. "Jeremiah got it for him when I first moved in. He thought it was hilarious. I don't think he ever expected Aaron to actually use it, though."

Aaron shrugged and turned to the women, showing off the apron in all its glory. "It's useful. And I kind of like the cats."

Jessica looked at her fiancé with the overly dreamy expression she seemed to wear every time she glanced his direction.

Then Aaron's phone buzzed, and Renee felt antici-pation build in her stomach as he fished the device out of his back pocket. It could be anyone, but...

"It's Jeremiah," Aaron said, confirming Renee's hope. "He wants to know if we need help today."

Please say yes, Renee thought at her sister.

Jessica nodded. "Yeah, that'd be great. I want us to work on getting that arch together and setting up things in the barn for the ceremony."

Renee was so excited, she almost missed everything Jessica said after "yeah." Once she soaked in her sister's words, though, she couldn't help but comment. "You're getting married in the barn?"

Jessica smiled at her. "Don't make fun of me. It'll be warm and dry in case it rains, and it's going to be re-ally pretty. Plus, this is Texas. If we *didn't* get married in the barn, people would talk."

Renee turned to Aaron. "Let me guess. You're going to wear cowboy boots, right?"

Aaron nodded proudly. "Oh yeah. It's going to be great."

Renee put a hand to her forehead. She felt like she was living in an alternate dimension. One full of giant silver belt buckles and saloons and horses. She missed the cold streets of New York City.

"I told Jeremiah to come by whenever," Aaron said to Jessica as he sat down with his own plate of food.

Renee's homesickness disappeared in a blink. She imagined them sneaking away together to continue where they'd left off the night before. There were some advantages to living in this alternate dimension, for a little while, at least.

Jeremiah showed up less than a half hour later, while Jessica and Aaron were washing the dishes. Aaron looked over his shoulder at his friend. "That was quick," he commented.

Jeremiah shrugged, but shot Renee a look that sent tendrils of fire snaking through her. "Might as well get the day started. It's not like I have anything else I want to do today."

Renee smiled at him, reading his message loud and clear. Jeremiah sat down beside her, making her pulse race. "Hi," he said, in an almost-conspiratorial whisper.

"Hey," she responded, feeling that they were saying so much more than perfunctory greetings. The space between them felt charged, like the air right before a lightning storm.

"Well," Aaron said, oblivious to the interactions going on behind him, "you missed breakfast, but I could fry a couple of eggs for you real quick."

"No thanks," he responded before turning back to Renee with a grin. "Did he wear his apron?"

She chuckled. "I have no idea how you managed to find an apron that god-awful."

His eyes lit up at the approval in her voice, and she almost melted into those dark pools of coffee. She was so close to him, she could see tiny flakes of lighter colors mixed in with the dark.

Renee was on her way to getting lost in them when Jessica came over to the table, wedding binder once more in hand. Renee forced herself to drag her attention away from the man beside her, trying to remember rule number one for the week. She hated to think about how obvious it seemed like they were being, and could only hope that either it wasn't as noticeable as she thought or Jessica was too wrapped up in wedding details to pay attention.

Her sister didn't seem to think anything was amiss, though, and Renee breathed a quiet sigh of relief. Jessica opened the binder to a diagram, and began explaining her vision for the ceremony. "We don't have the chairs yet, so that'll need to wait, but I want to get the arch put together and in place here—" she pointed to one end of the diagram "—and get the plants and strings of lights taken care of so I can be sure this layout will work."

Renee listened to her sister, but a large part of her brain—and all of her body—was focused on the man sitting so close to her. She could hear his breathing, and a shiver slid along her spine each time he breathed out, as her body remembered that hot breath in her ear while he touched her.

By the time Jessica closed the binder and the three of them stood, Renee felt hot and flushed, and the ache in her belly was clamoring for attention.

Aaron joined the group, and together the four of them trooped out to the barn. As they rounded the side of the house and the barn came into view, Renee stopped walking and took in the scene before her. She had to admit, it was a stunning location for a wedding.

The barn was a crisp clean white with wood trim, not the bright red she had expected. It sat long and regal, contrasting beautifully with the tall trees behind it. The clear blue sky only added to the picturesque view.

To make it even more enticing, Aaron and Jeremiah had reached the large barn door and were sliding it open. At this distance, she could see the muscles rippling under Jeremiah's shirt, and when he turned to look at her, brushing his hair out of his face, her knees nearly gave out.

Her design-trained eye reveled in the lines and colors of the scene before her, and her libido roared at the impossibly handsome man that dominated it. She wasn't sure which urge was stronger: the one telling her to throw herself at him or the one telling her to grab her computer and create the perfect spread for the image to adorn.

She wished she had a camera and her computer in her hands so she could give life to the image in her mind. And she wished she had nothing but Jeremiah, up close and completely to herself.

But now wasn't a time for any of that. She needed to help her sister and put aside all the distractions warring inside her.

As if to remind her of that, Jessica put her arm around Renee, pulling her close to her side. "See? It's better than you thought."

Renee nodded, leaned her weight on her sister and answered, "You win. It's beautiful. I won't make fun of you for getting married in this barn. Just don't wear a cowboy hat, okay? It won't match your dress."

Jessica kissed her on the cheek and started pulling

her toward the building. "I'm not making any promises," she answered.

Renee rolled her eyes and laughed, following her sister into the barn.

JEREMIAH WATCHED RENEE laughing with her sister. His muscles tensed just looking at her and he ached to touch her. He didn't know how, but he was going to find some way to get her alone.

Jessica's voice broke through the fog in his brain that Renee was so good at creating, and he wrenched his attention to her. "The arch goes over there," she explained, pointing to the far end of the building. "That's where the officiant will stand. We'll need to hang lights through the rafters and clean up the ground today. I may be getting married in a barn, but that doesn't mean I want hay stuck to me as I say my vows."

Aaron leaned in to his fiancée, speaking in a low voice that Jeremiah could nonetheless hear. "Having hay stuck to you isn't so bad. I like finding it in your hair after."

The way Jessica's cheeks flushed, Jeremiah was sure she was picturing a very specific incident. He hadn't thought of it, but of course they'd had sex in the barn. The way they couldn't keep their hands off each other, he imagined it would be difficult to find a place where they hadn't done it.

Their relationship had been one of the key causes of his change of heart regarding casual sex in the first place. If it was possible to find someone irresistible who you also loved being around outside of the bedroom day after day, shouldn't you try to find it?

He sneaked a glance at Renee. *Not her*, he told himself.

She was irresistible, sure. And they did seem to have a spark between them that went beyond just the physical, but there were some necessary ingredients missing to make this a forever thing.

The biggest one, of course, was that she clearly didn't want anything serious.

He pushed the thoughts aside, not liking where they were going.

Better to think about other things, like how to get Jessica and Aaron working on something somewhere else. Preferably not within hearing distance of the barn, because once he had Renee alone, he wanted to be able to hear her, and if she screamed out like he pictured, they were sure to break the first rule.

He smiled to himself at that.

RENEE KEPT HER eyes off Jeremiah despite the fire inside her and started moving one of the potted plants the two men had taken out of Jeremiah's truck the night before. She dragged it along the ground as Jessica directed her where to go and moved her own identical plant.

Renee had no idea what kind of plants they were, but the bright green leaves and little white flowers gave off an intoxicating scent that seemed almost erotic to her, in her current state.

She had to find a way to get him alone.

For two hours, though, she couldn't think of any way

to get Jessica and Aaron out of the barn. She moved plants, shifting them a couple of inches here and there until Jessica declared them perfect. Meanwhile, Jeremiah and Aaron were putting together the arch and bringing stacks of chairs into the building, leaning them against one side.

With each surreptitious glance at Jeremiah, more often than not catching him looking back at her, her body ached for him more. The air around her seemed too warm, and she began to feel desperate. She tied gauzy white fabric to each plant and silently begged Jessica to give her just a few minutes alone with him.

As if Renee had telepathically sent a message to her sister, Jessica stretched and said, "It's about time for a break, I think. Aaron and I will get some lunch together."

Renee didn't know if her sister expected her to follow them, but there was absolutely no way she was going to be leaving that barn.

She forced herself to nod as casually as she could and didn't look at Jeremiah. She wanted to know if he was as close to the breaking point as she was, but either it would be written all over his face, which would be bad, or it wouldn't. And she didn't want to see that. Better to wait.

Aaron walked over to Jessica and wrapped his arm around her waist. They were so easy and confident in their love for one another that it made something in Renee twinge. Not with jealousy, of course.

She didn't have time for a relationship like that, and besides, who could be as perfect for her as Aaron was for Jessica? Her eyes flitted over to Jeremiah. The only man she'd been at all attracted to in years couldn't possibly be anything other than a one-week romance, no matter how hard he made her heart pound.

No, that was definitely not something she wanted right now. She was happy for Jessica, but that was it.

Her inner monologue came to an abrupt end when two muscular arms slid around her the second Jessica and Aaron had walked out the door. His breath was hot against her ear, his voice low and deep, vibrating through her as he pressed his chest against her back. "I've been trying for two hours to come up with some way to get you alone. Are we still on?"

She answered by spinning around in his grasp and kissing him for all she was worth. There wasn't any time to spare. He kissed back just as enthusiastically, his tongue diving into her mouth in a way that made her fingers tingle. His teeth scraped against her lower lip as his hands moved under her shirt, and she felt like she was going to orgasm right there in the middle of the barn.

That thought brought her somewhat back to sanity, and she had enough of her mental faculties together to remember that they couldn't let Jessica and Aaron walk in on them like this.

Jeremiah was clearly thinking the same thing, because he pulled back slightly, breathing heavily, and nodded toward a nearby ladder. "How about we go up to the loft?"

She didn't need to be asked twice.

Renee climbed the ladder and found herself on a

platform twenty feet above the ground, the rafters of the barn low enough that she needed to duck when she walked under them. A large pile of Christmas lights sat in one corner, waiting to be strung around the room for the wedding.

While the rest of the barn was lit by the open door and windows, the loft was steeped in shadow, an oasis of evening even in the middle of the day. Renee stood and placed one hand on the rafter in front of her, looking out across the expanse below.

It was quiet and peaceful. The arch graced one end of the barn, tall and white and covered in greenery. The potted plants formed a walkway from the door to the arch, like escorts waiting to usher Jessica down the aisle.

She pictured her sister, beautiful and happy, walking down that aisle to the man she loved, and she felt that twinge again. As sure as she was that she didn't have time for any of that in her life, she had to admit that it would be nice to feel so loved.

And then Jeremiah was behind her again, his hands slipping across her stomach, and the scene dissolved. She leaned backward into him, and his hands roved higher. By the time they slid beneath her bra and found her breasts, her nipples were tight and aching for his touch.

His tongue and lips caressed her neck, sending jolts of electricity down her spine, and his fingers teased at her already-sensitive nipples, making her gasp with the intensity. She pressed her entire body back against him, feeling the bulge in his jeans. He growled deep in his throat at the contact, and she reveled in the powerful feeling that came with knowing that she drove him wild.

Then he rolled one nipple between his fingers and any sense of power disappeared. There was only need.

She turned to face him, her fingers dancing down across the muscles of his arms, all the way to the hem of his shirt. In a flash, she had his shirt over his head and soaked in the view of his naked torso. Even in the dim light, she could see that her fantasies hadn't done full justice to him. She moved one hand over his abs, marveling at the flesh below her fingers. He sucked in his breath at her touch. "You need to be careful doing that," he said, "because after being interrupted last night, I can't promise I have much control left."

She smiled wickedly and stroked his stomach again, making him groan. He said, "Remember on the ride from the airport, when I asked which one you were? You are most definitely the sexy one."

Renee laughed. In a lineup with her tall leggy sister and her perky blond best friend, Cindy, she highly doubted she would ever get labeled "the sexy one." But Jeremiah said it with such sincerity that a different kind of warmth flowed through her, this time headed straight for her heart.

That wasn't a good sign. Not if this was only going to be a one-week thing. She needed to bring it back to just physical. "You're even hotter than in my fantasies. I didn't even realize a guy could *have* an eight-pack."

With that, she ran her fingers along the waistline of his jeans, stopping at the button and working it open as quickly as she could. His stomach muscles shuddered again at her touch, and her stomach clenched in antici-pation. "What exactly occurred during these fantasies of yours?" he asked, his voice deep and full of the same desperate need she felt.

Renee felt a blush coming to her cheeks, but she an-swered honestly. "There have been a lot of fantasies since Vegas, and we've done so many things in them, it would take too long to go into detail."

He growled deep in his throat and leaned down to kiss her neck again. "Well, which one would you like to do now, in real life?"

That question had been running around her head for hours. Instead of answering with words, she lowered the zipper on his pants and reached in, her hand glid-ing across the smooth skin of his penis, rock-hard, as if it had been eagerly waiting for her touch.

Which it had been, she thought with a smile. He moaned, and his caresses suddenly turned urgent, his teeth grazing the skin of her neck and his hands knead-ing the tender flesh of her breasts until the clenching in her stomach had nearly reached a crescendo. One of his hands moved from her chest down toward her pants, and anticipation ran through her.

That was when they heard voices. Jessica and Aaron, getting louder as they approached the barn.

With another groan, this one of frustration, Jere-miah pulled himself away from her. The areas where his warm hands had been were suddenly exposed to the cold air. Jeremiah rubbed one hand across his face and gave her an exasperated look. "I'm going to kill Aaron, and he's not even going to know why."

Renee had to laugh, but she felt the same way about Jessica. Her stomach still felt tight and dissatisfied with the rude separation, and it didn't help that Jeremiah grabbed his shirt and tugged it back on.

"Renee? Jeremiah? Where are you two? Food's ready!" her sister called from somewhere below.

Jeremiah took a deep breath, gave Renee a grin and a wink, and leaned over the edge of the loft. "We're up here! Just working on untangling the lights so we can hang them up," he said, his voice much more light-hearted than Renee felt.

"That's such a good idea. Thanks, Jeremiah."

She couldn't see Jessica, but the genuine relief in her voice filled Renee with guilt. Her sister desperately wanted help getting everything ready for the wedding, and they had been seeing to their own desires instead.

Jeremiah gave her a look that said he was thinking the same thing, and they each rearranged their disheveled clothing without a word. Before they could start down the ladder, though, Renee said quietly, "I think we need to cool it, at least for today. I have to be here for Jessica, you know?"

Part of her prayed he would come up with an argument that would convince her otherwise, but he just sighed and nodded and she knew it was the right thing to do, no matter how delicious he looked.

He gave her a lopsided grin and shrugged one shoulder. "You just let me know when you can take time off from being a good sister and I'll be there."

His smile was so endearing she wanted to tackle him right there. But then he disappeared down the ladder and she took a deep breath of Jeremiah-free air and was able to strengthen her resolve before following him.

Jessica was waiting for them near the door, and they walked together to the house. Over sandwiches—ones that blew Renee's corner deli out of the water—Jessica discussed next steps.

"Since you two started on the lights," she said, pointing at Renee and Jeremiah, "you can finish untangling the lights, checking that all the bulbs work, and stringing them up through the rafters while Aaron and I meet with our reverend in town. Does that sound okay?"

Renee wanted to slap her forehead. Or Jessica's forehead. She wanted to be a helpful sister, but it was as if Jessica was *trying* to put her into situations that made it impossible. Now she was supposed to spend a bunch of unchaperoned time up in the loft with Jeremiah, and Jessica expected them to get anything done?

If she wasn't careful, only one thing would get done up there, and she was positive it wasn't on her sister's list.

Jeremiah gave her a brief glance that told her exactly where his mind had gone, and she pressed her hands against her legs under the table to stop them from jittering.

No, she told herself. They would have to get the lights taken care of first. If they finished and had time to spare, though...

Jeremiah couldn't wait for lunch to be over. All he'd wanted was more time up in the loft with Renee, and here was Jessica, handing him just that. Once they were back in the barn alone and climbing the ladder again, however, Renee went straight to the pile of lights and began tugging at them.

He wanted to make her forget all about the damn lights, but he thought of the conversation they had had before lunch. She was just trying to be a good sister, and he didn't begrudge her that, no matter how much the pressure in his jeans protested. He sat down beside her and grabbed a knotted section of lights and set to work.

"We need to get this done for Jessica," she told him.

He hoped she meant they needed to do this *first*, because their last two encounters had left him desperate for more, and if he had to go home without getting to touch her again, he thought he might go crazy. Still, he nodded and set to work.

After just a few seconds of silence, the tension in the air became too much for him. The quiet gave him too much time to think about the delights they could be having, and it made him feel precariously close to throwing down the lights and pressing her against the rough boards they were sitting on.

"So," he began, not really sure what he was going to say, "we've established that you're the workaholic one and the sexy one. What else are you?"

If he wasn't allowed to kiss and touch her, he could at least learn more about her. She smiled and shook her head, but didn't glance up from her task. "*A*, I'm not the sexy one by any stretch of the imagination. And *B*," she continued before he could argue, "*workaholic* sounds way too negative. I prefer the term *driven*."

He laughed. "I'll let the workaholic thing go, but

you're definitely the sexy one. It's cute that you don't see it."

She shook her head again, but he could tell she was flattered. He hoped she understood that he wasn't just saying that; her captivating eyes and the curve of her smile set his blood on fire. Not to mention the perfect size of her breasts and an ass that made him hard just thinking about it.

He ripped his thoughts back to more appropriate aspects of her. If he had to sit next to her without groping her or going insane with lust, he'd need to control those thoughts. "I bet you're the funny, clever one," he said, hoping she didn't notice how he shifted position so his erection wouldn't be too painful.

She shrugged. "Very few people would consider me to be the funny one. My sense of humor is, let's say, more unique than Jessica's."

As the guy who was always considered the entertainment of the group, he had to hear more. She continued, "Jessica is better at being sarcastic. I'm more…punny."

"Punny? I don't think that's a word. Give me an example."

She sighed, and he could tell even in the dim light that she was blushing. "You really don't want to hear my jokes, I promise."

"Tell me just one. Please?" he begged.

He tried to pay attention to the lights, but he was so interested to hear her response that it was hard to do much more than fumble around with them.

"Fine," she answered, sounding both amused and exasperated. "But you asked for it."

She paused for a second, then, "Did you hear the one about the three holes in the ground? No? Well, well, well…"

He groaned and laughed simultaneously, delighted. "That was so corny."

She smiled and shrugged again in that way she had. "I told you. Please don't ask me for any more, because that was my best one."

He thought about the terrible joke again, chuckling while he tried to come up with a new topic of conversation.

He wanted to know more about her, everything about her, but he didn't know what to ask. He looked down at the lights and thought about how she'd taken a break from her beloved work to come decorate for her sister's wedding. "Have you and Jessica always been close?"

Renee smiled, but she kept her eyes down on the lights. "We've never had any big fights or anything, but we weren't very close until our dad got sick."

Jeremiah nodded. He knew the story about their father and his long illness. He'd died two years ago, the same weekend that Jessica and Aaron had met. Jeremiah wished he hadn't reminded Renee of it—the way her voice grew quieter as she said it made him ache inside.

She continued, "We both pitched in to take care of him, so it helped us connect a bit more than we had as kids."

He tried to turn the conversation away from her dad. "Why weren't you two better friends when you were kids? Was she a mean older sister?"

Renee brushed her hair behind her ear as she thought.

It was a simple unconscious move, but something about it struck him as particularly endearing. "No, she was fine. We're just different people. Always have been."

Before he could ask another question, she shot one back at him, asking how long he'd been friends with Aaron.

The time passed quickly as they chatted. After two and a half hours, they had untangled the lights, checked for missing or blown bulbs, and begun stringing them up. They'd also told each other about their childhoods, first crushes (his, a girl in his third grade class named Claire Isaacs, hers, Jonathon Taylor Thomas from *Home Improvement*), favorite movies (*The Truman Show* and *When Harry Met Sally*, though Renee confessed she secretly loved *High School Musical*), and she'd gotten him to admit that yes, the songs from *Frozen* were actually pretty catchy and he knew more of the words than a man his age should. "My niece loves that movie," he tried to explain, "and we had to watch it at least twenty times the last time I visited."

Renee nodded and said, "Sure, I believe you. Your *niece* likes it," but her smile was more like a Cheshire cat grin than anything else, and he loved it.

In fact, he loved almost everything about her. Her laugh, her terrible puns, the way she raised one eyebrow when he said something she thought was strange.

He'd been pretty sure before, but now he was positive: this thing wasn't going to end easily for him at all. He was getting further and further from casual sex, and there wasn't any way out that he was willing to take. He was already hooked on her, and without some sort of drastic change over the coming week, he would be left alone and worse off than before once she went back to New York.

RENEE STOOD ON the edge of the loft, holding a rope of lights bunched up in one hand. When she tossed it, it unraveled as it flew through the air. Jeremiah, standing on a ladder several feet away, deftly caught the end of the string and began circling it through a rafter above him. They had been working for hours, and she thought it would be torture to be so close to him for so long without finishing what they'd started.

In a way it was, but talking to him had been pretty amazing, actually. He was as pleasant and amusing as Jessica and Aaron made him out to be, but more than that, too. He was sweet and confident, and there was an air of honesty about him that was incredibly refreshing. It wasn't something she saw a lot in New York.

She plugged in the final strings of bulbs and climbed down from the loft. She and Jeremiah stood just to the side of the door in order to survey their work. The barn was still romantically dim, but the bright dots of light threaded through the rafters added a fairy-tale quality to the whole place. She hoped Jessica would like it.

"We're done," she said, not sure how to transition from lighthearted conversation to making out. She suddenly felt awkward around him.

"It was an en-*light*-ening experience," he said, grinning and lifting his eyebrows. "Get it? Because of the lights," he added. "That's your kind of joke, right?"

She laughed and leaned into him, meaning to bump

him playfully with her shoulder, but he wrapped his arm around her and pulled her tight before she could do so, and in an instant they were kissing.

Renee fell into the kiss, letting her mind blank as he enfolded her.

Then she froze as she heard Jessica gasp. *Oh shit*, she thought, pushing away from Jeremiah.

Her sister stood in the doorway, not ten feet from them, looking up at the ceiling. Relief flooded through Renee as she realized Jessica hadn't noticed them. She took a deep breath and looked at Jeremiah, whose facial expression had gone from panic to amusement in the two seconds it took for him to comprehend what had just happened.

They smiled at each other and Jeremiah shook his head in exasperation. She felt the same way. Would they ever get enough time alone together to actually make something happen?

Renee shrugged back and turned her attention to her sister. "You like it?"

Jessica nodded, still gazing at the room before her. "You two did an amazing job. Thank you so much!"

As frustrated as she was at yet another interruption, Renee was happy she'd done something for her sister instead of being completely selfish and using all that time to indulge in fantasies.

Well, somewhat happy.

Anyway, she was sure they'd find time.

Jessica looped her arm around Renee and squeezed. "I owe you big-time." Renee thought about the interrupted kiss. *You sure do,* she thought.

"I think that's enough work on the barn for today," Jessica said, to Renee's chagrin. "Let's head back to the house. We can spend the rest of the day double-checking the menu and going over seating arrangements."

Renee knew her sister was meticulous, but this seemed a touch overboard. "I thought there were only thirty guests or something. Do you really need seating arrangements? Can't people just sit wherever?"

Jessica looked at her like she was crazy, and Renee knew this wasn't a battle she could possibly win. "Seating arrangements it is," she said before Jessica could explain to her exactly why they were so important.

It was her sister's wedding, after all. Whatever made her happy.

Jessica smiled. "I know you think I'm neurotic," she began, and Renee didn't disagree, "but it'll all be worth it, I'm sure."

With that, Jessica gestured toward the door. "Come on. You two have spent all day in this barn. Let's go back to the house and relax a bit."

She led the way out. The moment Jessica was past the door, Jeremiah leaned in close to Renee and murmured, "That woman must have a spidey sense or something. If that's going to happen all week, I don't think I'll survive."

Renee nodded and followed her sister, trying not to feel too disappointed.

6

JEREMIAH WATCHED RENEE walking ahead of him, captivated by the way her jeans hugged her butt. He didn't think his body could take much more of this.

In the house, Jessica pulled Renee into the living room, binder in hand. Renee gave him one last glance before disappearing from view, and then she was gone. He didn't think Jessica expected him to follow, but he was going to do it anyway, when Aaron walked out of the hallway and came toward his friend. "Thanks for all the help today. I think getting all that done eased Jessica's mind some. You must've been really bored to want to come by today and work on wedding stuff."

Jeremiah didn't trust himself to respond. Aaron knew him too well, and he was worried that anything he said might sound suspicious.

Aaron didn't notice. He said, "Well, tomorrow the girls are going into town so Renee can do a dress fitting and cake tasting, so you're off the hook for wedding stuff."

Jeremiah tried not to let his frustration show. The week was just getting started and he was already down a day, and for no good reason. Really, the only good reason would be something along the lines of saving puppies or getting a limb amputated, and even then he was pretty sure he could work around it. But there was nothing he could do. It wasn't like he could say anything.

He hated secrets.

"I thought you and Jessica had decided your cake flavors already," he responded, for lack of anything else to say.

"We did, a month ago, but Jessica wants to be sure that we made the right choice. And she wants Renee to try them so she can get input from someone who would tell her honestly if the flavors we picked are good."

"And that's not you?"

"With cake, I'm completely honest, but I guess my bar is set too low or something because I thought we should order every flavor they make. Seriously, we should buy wedding cakes from this shop as a weekly thing."

Jeremiah couldn't do anything about that day, then, but he wasn't about to lose any more of them. "Well, think of something for me to do on Monday. The wedding will be here before you know it."

"Actually, I have to go pick up the rings on Monday. Want to go with me? You'll be holding on to them anyway."

"Sure. How about I come over for breakfast and then we can go."

Aaron smiled at his friend. "You want free food out of this deal?"

"Hey, a man's got to eat," Jeremiah replied, but he wasn't thinking about the food.

The more time he spent in their house, the more time he got around Renee and the more chances he had to be alone with her. If he could come up with a plausible reason, he'd live there for the next seven days. With Renee right across the hall…well, they would definitely be able to come up with a few fun ways to spend their nights.

Since that didn't seem feasible, he would take what he could get.

RENEE WAS SITTING with her sister on the couch reviewing the menu when Jeremiah and Aaron walked in. Aaron sat beside Jessica in a space so small that she was nearly sitting on his lap—which he didn't seem to mind in the least—and Jeremiah grabbed a chair nearby.

She wished she could be sitting in his lap at the moment, but instead had to fight to hide the way her body reacted the moment he walked into the room. This fun idea of secretly indulging in her fantasies was rapidly becoming torture, but she didn't see any way around that if she wanted to have her cake and eat it, too. And Jeremiah was the most addictive cake she'd ever seen.

"Does everyone think corn bread is the right choice over sweet rolls?" Jessica asked, looking around at the small group.

"Corn bread matches the whole Texas country theme

you've got going on," Renee answered, trying not to sound amused.

Jessica seemed relieved by Renee's answer, which just made it harder for Renee to keep a straight face. Jessica had only been in Texas for two years, but she seemed to have jumped on the country bandwagon wholeheartedly as soon as she and Aaron started living together.

"I love corn bread," Jeremiah answered. "In fact, if it's really great corn bread, I might end up eating way too much of it, leaving your other guests to starve and making myself sick in the process, effectively ruining the entire—Ow!"

Jeremiah rubbed the spot on his bicep where Aaron had just punched him. He and Renee shared a grin as Aaron settled back into his spot on the couch.

Aaron wrapped his arm around Jessica, pulling her tight against him. "The corn bread will be great," he said, kissing her temple.

Jessica gave her fiancé that dreamy smile again, then turned to Jeremiah. "No joking allowed about anything wedding-related," she told him pointedly.

"I never agreed to that," Jeremiah responded, flashing Renee another grin that made her weak in the knees.

Jessica saw the smile and wheeled on her sister. "And don't you start conspiring with him, Renee."

"I didn't do anything," Renee answered, holding up her hands in innocence.

"Let's keep it that way," Jessica retorted, crossing her arms and snuggling back into Aaron's chest, trying to look as serious as she could. "I can still un-bridesmaid you, you know."

Jeremiah grinned. "She's stuck with me because I'm the only groomsman, but she's still got Cindy if she kicks you out. You're expendable."

Jessica nodded in agreement and Renee laughed.

"No conspiring," Renee promised.

It wasn't precisely true, Renee thought, but not in the way Jessica was thinking, so there was no reason to say anything about that.

THE REST OF the afternoon passed in much the same way, with Jessica trying to get serious answers and Jeremiah and Renee alternating teasing her. Finally, Renee set a hand on the binder. "It all sounds perfect, Jessica. You did a great job."

Jessica took a deep breath and closed the binder, to Renee's relief. She had come up with a way to get Jeremiah alone again, and been waiting nearly an hour to implement it. She stood and stretched, glancing sideways at Jeremiah. "I think I need to take a walk."

Right on cue, Jeremiah jumped up. "Me, too. I can show you around the property."

Excitement welled inside Renee as she imagined them out under the trees together. It was a little cool out, but she was sure they could think of ways to stay warm.

"That's a great idea," Jessica said. "We have some time before we need to start getting dinner ready. Let's all go for a walk."

Renee bit her lip in frustration. Her sister was going

to be the death of her. Either that or she would be the death of her sister.

Jessica and Aaron led the way out of the room. Renee looked over at Jeremiah, who was shaking his head in disbelief. Without a word, they followed the other two out of the house and across a wide expanse of lawn. Jessica started talking about the acreage and features of the property like a motivated real estate agent, but Renee only half listened. Most of her mind was focused on Jeremiah walking beside her. She could almost feel him, like an electric charge that was building up, about to explode.

She wondered if it was possible to burst into flames from sexual frustration.

When they were nearly at a paddock full of horses, Jeremiah grabbed her hand and pulled her behind a tree. The moment they were out of sight, she leaned in for a kiss. It was hardly any privacy, but at this point beggars couldn't be choosers.

Jeremiah leaned away, though. In answer to the look she gave him, he said, "Sorry, but if I get any closer to you I won't be able to control myself, and I'm pretty sure Jessica would notice if we started having sex up against this tree."

Renee's attention shifted to the tree. Maybe if they were really quiet...

She couldn't believe she was even considering that. She needed to get laid. Bad.

Jeremiah continued, his voice husky with pent-up desire, "It doesn't look like we'll be able to see each other tomorrow—" the tree was looking better and better— "but I'll be here Monday, and I will come up with a way for us to get alone that afternoon. Several ways, just in case your sister pulls something like this again. Because I don't know if I can take much more of this."

Renee nodded, and Jeremiah pushed a strand of hair behind her ear, leaving a trail of fire where his fingers touched her skin.

Monday. She could probably survive until then.

After one last long look at each other, they broke apart and came out from behind the tree, walking casually up to where Jessica and Aaron stood fifty feet away.

"Where'd you disappear to?" Jessica asked when they approached.

"I was telling Renee about the trees on the property," Jeremiah answered.

Jessica nodded and turned back to the horses. She began telling Renee about them, giving each one's name and breed. Renee tried to pay attention, but her mind was too distracted for her to care much about horses.

When they got back to the house, it was time to start dinner. Renee didn't even dare to hope that she and Jeremiah would have some time to themselves, and she was right. "Jeremiah, can you make your sauce for the pork chops?" Jessica asked the moment they stepped in the door.

"What should I do?" Renee asked when she realized she'd be sitting alone in the other room if she didn't volunteer to help.

Since Renee didn't have any actual cooking skills, she was given salad duty. In no time, the four of them were sitting around the table, one or the other occasionally going to check on something as dinner cooked.

Once everything was nearly ready, Renee set the

table, making sure that she and Jeremiah would be sitting beside each other. If that was the only way she was going to get close to him, by God, she was going to take advantage of it.

AFTER WASHING HIS HANDS, Jeremiah walked back to the table that was now prepared for dinner. He paused for only a moment when he realized that Renee had placed them next to one another, then went to his spot with what he hoped was nonchalance. They would be under the gaze of Jessica and Aaron the whole time, but at least he could hope for some opportunities to brush against Renee's arm, even touch her hand under the table. At least it would be something.

And then Renee slipped her hand into his lap, rubbing against his upper thigh, obliterating any chance Jeremiah had of staying under control.

"Are you okay, Jeremiah?" Jessica asked, looking concerned.

No surprise there. He probably looked like he'd choked on his own tongue, which had very nearly happened when he realized what Renee was doing. Her hand inched higher ever-so-slightly, and it took everything he had not to react.

"Yeah, I'm fine," he said, hoping his voice didn't sound as weird to them as it did in his ears. "I just swallowed wrong." He coughed to give his story credibility and prayed the couple didn't notice he hadn't eaten anything yet.

Jessica went back to her food and Jeremiah relaxed a little bit, giving Renee a quick glance out of the corner of his eye. She had her water glass up to her mouth, but he could tell by the tilt of her lips that she was having difficulty suppressing a laugh.

Two could play at that game.

Luckily, the table was big and solid, large enough to fit twice as many people, and high enough to hide any activity going on below. He intended to take complete advantage of it. As he leaned forward to grab the butter for his roll with one hand, the other rubbed suggestively against the denim of Renee's jeans—first on her thigh, then moving quickly to her center. He knew the pressure had hit home when a tiny gasp burst from her. It was his turn to hide a smile behind a water glass.

Jessica and Aaron were fortunately so absorbed in conversation—he had no idea what they were talking about, but whatever it was clearly interested them—that they didn't notice anything odd about what was happening on the other side of the table. And it was a good thing for him, too, because Renee answered back with a foot riding so far up his leg she had to be double-jointed or something.

That thought made the room feel much too warm. He needed air, but there was no way he'd be getting up from that table. Not while Renee was still doing things that might make him implode.

By the end of dinner, he was so hot and bothered that it took several minutes before he was able to stand.

Long past dark, Jeremiah left, his body aching for release. He didn't know if that woman was sent from heaven or hell, but either way, all he could think about was the next time he'd be able to get her alone. All the things he wanted to do to her, should the opportunity come up, raced through his mind as he eased himself into his truck for the long, lonely ride home.

THE NEXT MORNING, Renee stood under the spray from the showerhead, splashing the hot water on her face. She knew she had to pull herself together—she and Jessica would be tasting cake in two hours—but she felt terrible. Her night had been restless, her brain conjuring fantasy after steamy fantasy of Jeremiah. If she wasn't able to fulfill some of them soon, she was pretty sure her body would seize up and send her to the hospital out of spite.

She still couldn't believe she'd been so brazen during dinner the night before. What had she been thinking, playing footsie like that, with Jessica right there?

She hadn't been thinking at all, plain and simple. Jeremiah was so damn sexy that being near him made her brain shut off.

And the worst part was, she couldn't regret one moment of it. Just thinking of his hand sliding up her thigh sent her blood pressure skyrocketing, and she couldn't wait for him to touch her again. Whenever that would be.

Rinsing her hair, she pictured what it would be like to have Jeremiah in the shower with her. Soapy. Wet. Naked. So very naked.

She bit her lip in frustration. How much more of this could she take?

One day, she told herself. If she survived today, Jeremiah had promised that the next one would make up for it. In the meantime, though, she would need to do *something* to get her through the day.

Her hand slid down her body, edging through the dark thatch of curls covering her sex, her finger sliding over her clitoris as she allowed her mind's eye to return to the picture of Jeremiah in the shower with her.

Her body was so ready after all the sexual torment of the past few days that it only took a couple of minutes for her to shudder as an orgasm shot through her. The tension in her body eased, but didn't disappear entirely. She had a feeling she would need Jeremiah in the flesh, and *only* the flesh, in order to completely satisfy her.

By the time she got downstairs, she had cooled down enough to face her sister and the day before her. The sexless, Jeremiah-less day.

At least there would be cake.

RENEE STOOD IN front of the mirror, taking one last look at her dress. She had gotten it tailored weeks before, but Jessica had asked her to try it on one last time at her bridal boutique, so here she was. The seamstress, a plump, grandmotherly, silver-haired woman, studied the satin dress carefully. "It's a perfect fit," she declared at last, "and quite lovely on you, dear."

Renee glanced at her reflection. To her surprise, the color didn't seem to contrast quite as terribly with her hair as she had first thought. And all the cake they'd eaten that morning hadn't attached itself to her hips quite yet. She didn't look bad at all.

"I told you it was fine," Renee called to her sister, who was hidden from view by a large curtain.

"It never hurts to check," Jessica called back, her voice muffled.

The seamstress smiled at her. She was clearly familiar with Jessica. The curtain slid back and her sister stepped out of the dressing room, and their attention shifted to the woman in the beautiful white wedding dress.

The lace halter of the dress showed off Jessica's tan skin, the bodice hugged her curves and the skirt flowed to the floor in waves of fabric. Renee felt a pang of jealousy for her sister's height and perfect proportions. She was certain no wedding dress would ever look that good on her.

Not that she was anywhere near needing or wanting one, she reminded herself. There was too much to do before that even became an issue.

Jeremiah's easy smile flashed through her mind, but she pushed it away. Thinking about sexy flings while in a wedding shop was a definite no-no.

Jessica stood in front of the mirror. "What do you think?" she asked her sister.

Renee wanted to hug her, but was afraid of wrinkling the dress, so she made do with a squeeze of her hand. "You look so beautiful."

Jessica sighed and ran her hands across the silky skirt, that dreamy look back in her eyes. The one she had whenever she looked at Aaron. Renee had that feeling in her gut again, the not-jealousy one.

"It looks like it's ready to take home," Jessica said, turning her back to the mirror and eyeing the train.

Renee nodded. Jessica did one last thorough check,

then started moving back toward her dressing room. "I better get this off before something happens to it," she said.

Renee looked around at the sterile environment. "What could possibly happen to it here?"

"I don't know. Somebody could walk in with tomato sauce and trip and spill it all over me or something."

Renee didn't say a word. There was no point commenting every single time her sister worried about something ridiculous.

As Renee moved toward her own dressing room, her sister turned back to look at her with a smile. "Remember when we were kids and would play dress-up wedding with that old white dress of Mom's?"

Renee chuckled at the memory. "Yeah. That was fun."

Jessica's smile widened. "We'd take turns being the bride and the bridesmaid."

"You were really bad at taking turns. You always wanted to be the bride."

"Well, I've grown up and gotten much better at taking turns."

Renee wasn't sure exactly what Jessica was talking about, but she had a bad feeling as to where this was going. "What do you mean?"

"It's your turn," Jessica said, pointing to the dressing room.

Renee moved the curtain that served as the door to her dressing room, and there was a giant mass of white fabric that hadn't been there before. "Oh no," she muttered.

"Oh yes," Jessica responded, triumphant.

"I'm not putting that on." What was Jessica thinking?

"Come on. I saw it here months ago and thought of you. Please? For me?" Jessica begged.

Renee cautiously moved closer to the dress, as if she was afraid it would bite. The strapless bodice sparkled, and the full skirt looked light and airy. "Rhinestones make you think of me?"

"Just try it on," Jessica demanded.

Renee pressed her lips together. She'd do it, but only because it was her sister's wedding week and she was trying to be nice. Not because the fabric was beautiful or she was at all curious how it would look on her.

One of the saleswomen followed her into the dressing room and helped her into what looked like miles of fabric. "When are you getting married?" the woman asked.

"I'm not," Renee answered as she wriggled herself into place. "My sister is making me do this."

The woman began lacing up the back and adjusting the dress until it sat comfortably on Renee's hips. "Well, I think she picked the perfect dress for you. Now you know which one to get whenever you and Mr. Right decide to settle down."

Renee had to force herself not to shake her head. Clearly the woman was trying to make a sale, because there was no way she could pull off a dress like this. On some tall curvy woman it might be beautiful, but she was sure that she'd look like a little kid playing dress-up, just like she and Jessica used to do.

She stepped out of the dressing room, hoping Jessica

would let her change back into her regular clothing as soon as she saw how ridiculous this dress looked on her.

Jessica was standing there in jeans and a T-shirt. When she saw Renee, her eyes widened.

"You really thought I could pull this off?" Renee asked, gesturing at the full skirt that poufed out from her hips.

Jessica just pointed at the mirrors. Renee sighed and walked over to them. Then her breath caught in her throat as she took in her reflection. She didn't look silly at all. The rhinestones on the corset top and the wide tulle skirt should have looked like too much, but somehow it just looked elegant and...well...

Beautiful, she admitted to herself. She looked beautiful.

Renee couldn't stop staring at her image in the mirror. Jessica beamed at her. "I knew you'd love it."

Renee couldn't deny it.

Finally, reality set in. What was she doing goggling at herself in a wedding dress? She wasn't getting married. Not even close.

She looked at her sister. "I'm not getting married anytime soon, Jessica. So why did you want me to try on this dress?"

"For one, I was sure it'd be perfect on you," Jessica answered. Then her expression became more serious. "And for another, I think you're hiding from any opportunity to find a relationship that makes you happy. I thought maybe this would help."

Renee didn't know what to say, so she just continued to look at her reflection. Was her overly blunt sister right? "I'm too busy for a relationship, Jess."

Jessica rolled her eyes. "You choose to be too busy. Don't think I haven't noticed, even from Texas. You never go out on dates, and you work every chance you get. You've been doing this to yourself for years now. Have you thought about why?"

Renee tried to push away her sister's words, but it was hard. She reminded herself why she worked so hard, and how it was finally paying off with her dream job so close she could smell it.

Those thoughts didn't stop the roiling in her stomach, though. Maybe she'd eaten too many cake samples that morning, she told herself.

She wasn't sure she believed it.

With difficulty, she tore her eyes away from her reflection. "Can I put on my regular clothes now?"

She tried to sound exasperated, but by the look on Jessica's face as she nodded, Renee doubted it worked.

After changing back into her jeans and T-shirt, Renee left the store with Jessica, wedding dress in tow. Renee said nothing about the other dress, but her sister's triumphant expression didn't leave her face the entire way back to the ranch.

Renee felt unsettled about the whole thing. Even the perfect dress and Jessica's words shouldn't change her feelings about marriage and all that, but for some reason, she didn't feel nearly as terrified by the prospect as she used to. She was going to be too busy with her new job to even consider a serious relationship, but the usual relief that came with that idea was no longer there. It felt more like resignation.

Maybe her sister was right. That thought left a bad taste in her mouth and she pushed it away.

She seemed to be doing that a lot lately.

When they walked inside Jessica and Aaron's home, Renee flopped on the couch, exhausted. She felt like she'd had more cake and self-reflection than anyone should on one day.

Jessica sat beside her, and Renee could feel her stare. She opened her eyes and waited for whatever her sister was going to say.

"I know it's been a long, wedding-focused day, but do you mind going through the receipts with me to make sure I haven't missed anything?" Jessica asked, a pleading look in her eyes.

Renee was absolutely positive her sister hadn't missed anything, but nodded anyway. At least Jessica didn't seem inclined to discuss the dress or Renee's relationships or anything like that. She wasn't sure she would've been able to take much more of that in one day.

"Great!" Jessica exclaimed, bouncing up to grab her binder, a large manila envelope and her laptop. She passed the computer over to Renee. "I'll read off an item, and you can go through the folder on my desktop. I have a few paper copies," she said, pointing to the envelope, "but almost everything is digital."

Renee placed the laptop on her legs and began to open the folder labeled Wedding when something else caught her eye—a document titled "City Girl, Country Life." While Jessica flipped through her binder in search of the right page, Renee opened the document and began reading.

Her eyes skimmed down through the pages. It was an article all about transitioning to life on a ranch. And it was good. Renee could easily imagine it as one of the articles she'd design spreads for back in New York.

"Did you write this?" she asked, turning the screen toward her sister. Jessica looked up, confused, but she blushed the moment she saw what Renee had opened.

"Oh, that's nothing. Just something I wrote when I first moved here," Jessica said, trying to lean over Renee to close it.

Renee pulled the laptop back, out of her sister's reach, relieved to find something new to focus on that had nothing to do with weddings or sexy cowboys. She was finally in an area where she felt confident. "This is great, Jess. You should submit it for publishing. I bet *Empire* would run it. We're always looking for pieces with interesting perspectives."

Jessica waved her fingers in front of her face, as if trying to clear the air around her. "I don't think so. It was just for fun. I'm an editor, not a writer, remember?"

Renee pointed at the screen. "Looks to me like you're both."

Jessica grabbed the computer from Renee and closed the document before opening the wedding folder. "*Anyway*, back to the receipts."

Renee didn't say anything else about the piece, but she decided that she would get her sister to submit it to the magazine before the end of the week.

They spent an hour going through every item, and as expected, everything was in order. "I don't know what you're so worried about," Renee told her sister as they stood and stretched. "You've planned it all in excruciating detail. At this point, it doesn't seem like there's anything you could have missed."

Jessica nodded and held her beloved binder tight to her chest. "I know, but I just have this feeling that something's going to go wrong, and I'm trying to catch it before the big day."

Renee put her hand on her sister's shoulder. "You've got it all taken care of. Just enjoy this time, okay?"

Jessica nodded, but she still didn't seem reassured. Renee shrugged and began climbing the stairs to her room. She'd tried for years to stop her neurotic sister from worrying, but it never worked. Meanwhile, she had enough on her plate, between helping with the wedding, preparing for her new job and trying to simultaneously have a sexy tryst with Jeremiah and keep it totally under wraps.

As she dropped onto the bed and smelled his already-familiar scent, she finally allowed herself to think about him and their few short stolen kisses. He had been on her mind all day, but it was only now that she let herself truly delve into it.

Renee knew they would never be in a serious relationship, but she couldn't stop her heart from fluttering when she thought of him. Something was different now, though. Ignoring her sister's earlier words and trying to forget that dress was harder than she liked.

She grimaced and sat up, rubbing her face with her

hands. Was that going to ruin her one chance to have a spectacular time with the sexiest man she'd ever met?

Renee hoped not, but it was all getting tied up in her head, and she didn't like that. She grabbed her laptop and opened a page she'd been designing for a future issue. At least work could keep her mind off things. Life was always a little clearer when she was working on a project.

For the rest of the evening, Renee worked on the page, tweaking it until it was close to perfect. When she went down to eat, Jessica said nothing about their earlier conversation, to Renee's relief.

By the time she finished the page, it was late enough to go to bed, and Renee pulled up the covers, ready to be done with this day.

Jeremiah had promised that tomorrow would be their chance, but suddenly she felt more nervous than excited. The whole thing suddenly seemed like a train wreck waiting to happen, and she didn't know if she had the power to prevent it.

7

JEREMIAH LOOKED OUT the window of his house, watching as the color of the sky slowly shifted from pink and gold to blue. Yesterday had been frustrating, to say the least, but it was finally over. Today was going to be different, he was sure. After he and Aaron went to pick up the rings, he would finally get some real time alone with Renee.

He thought of her smile, the way her hands felt pressed against his chest, and his body reacted immediately. He leaned his forehead against the cool glass and closed his eyes. The same thing had been happening over and over since he'd first seen her. He just hoped that he would be able to work whatever this was out of his system by the end of the week.

Aaron's text from yesterday popped unbidden into his head. Aaron had thought it was hilarious that Jessica managed to get Renee to try on a poufy princess wedding dress, but it wasn't that funny to Jeremiah.

He didn't really know how he felt about it, but amused definitely wasn't one of the competing emotions.

RENEE WAS JUST finishing yet another delicious breakfast when Jeremiah walked in. She'd been anxious all morning, waiting for him to arrive so he and Aaron could go pick up the wedding rings, but his sudden appearance still made her almost choke on her bacon. She felt her face go warm. Why was it that every time she saw him, a jolt went through her entire body?

He smiled at her with one eyebrow raised, and she knew he was enjoying her inability to control her reactions. Impulsively, she dabbed her finger into the syrup on her plate and sucked it off, not taking her eyes away from him. The grin fell away from his face and his mouth opened slightly as he watched. A feeling of power coursed through her. She wasn't the only one who could be thrown off balance.

Any hesitations that might have resulted from her conversations with Jessica the day before disappeared as she felt her blood surge. Whatever her issues were, she wasn't going to let them—or her sister's opinion of them—stop her from taking advantage of this once-in-a-lifetime opportunity.

Aaron jumped up from the table. "Great. I'm glad you came over early. Let's get going."

Renee saw disappointment flash across Jeremiah's face. "Will the store even be open this early?"

"No, but there are a few other things we need to take care of. That's okay, right?"

Renee knew there was nothing he could say that wouldn't give away that something was going on, so he shrugged one shoulder and turned to leave back through the door he'd just entered from, but not without sending a look of regret her way.

Renee was simultaneously disappointed that he had to leave so quickly and secretly pleased that he had tried to come over early so he could spend time with her.

And then he was gone, and the warmth that had flowed into the kitchen when he arrived disappeared, too.

She remembered his promise about the afternoon, and a thrill ran through her. She would just need to occupy herself for a few hours.

Renee turned to her sister. "What's on the docket today?"

Jessica looked excited, like she'd hoped Renee would ask her that. "We need to create the centerpieces and wedding favors," she said, holding up a bag of what looked like art supplies.

Renee waited for more of an explanation. She didn't have to wait long. "We need to spray paint wine bottles," Jessica continued, "and decorate some flower pots. Once they're dry, we'll be able to start adding the plants and arranging them on a test table."

Renee smiled at her sister. It sounded more fun than going over receipts or seating charts again, at least.

Three hours later, Renee brushed the hair out of her face with the back of one paint-speckled hand. She looked over the sea of flower pots spread out before her in varying stages of completion. Some were still their original terra-cotta color, others were bright white and still others had painted stenciled flowers drying along the top. Jessica sat beside her, cheerfully dabbing paint onto yet another pot.

"WHAT DO YOU THINK?" Aaron asked, turning the tiny box so the diamonds on the wedding band nestled inside glittered in the light.

"I think I'm the luckiest girl in the world!" Jeremiah exclaimed.

Aaron rolled his eyes as Jeremiah laughed at his own joke. "Is it too late to get a new best man?"

Jeremiah waved off the question. "You know Jessica will love it."

"I hope so."

"Stop worrying. At this rate, you're both going to have breakdowns, and I don't want to be the one picking up the pieces."

Jeremiah took one last look at the ring as Aaron handed the box back to the jeweler. It was a strange thought, his best friend getting married. They had gone through childhood and wild young adult years together, and now Aaron was officially moving into the next stage. The wife-and-kids stage.

And Jeremiah was happy for him, even as he wondered when he'd be moving into that stage, too.

The sexy redhead, never too far from his mind, resurfaced again. She wasn't looking for anything serious. He knew that.

But he was an optimist. Maybe by the end of the week it could turn into something more.

RENEE LOOKED IN the mirror, checking to make sure she'd gotten all the paint off her face. Her stomach roiled in anticipation. Jeremiah could be back at any time, and then they'd enact whatever plan he had. And she could finally play out a few of her fantasies.

She suppressed the urge to dance around her room.

As Renee straightened up, her cell phone began to ring from the bedside table. She could only think of one person who might call her today, and a surge of either excitement or fear shot through her. Renee picked up her phone and looked at the screen. It was Patty, just like she thought. Nervous tension knotted inside her. What if it was bad news? What if they'd found someone else to take the position?

She took a deep breath and answered. "Hello?"

"Hi, Renee, it's Patty. I just got out of the meeting. I told them you were perfect for my position and recommended that they have you step in when I leave."

She paused, and Renee thought she might have a heart attack before Patty told her what happened.

"They trust my opinion, Renee. We'll iron out the details when you get back."

Breath whooshed out of Renee's lungs. Relief flooded her. This was actually going to happen.

"They just want to see some of your work, pages that haven't been edited by anyone else, to make sure they're happy with what you do. You'll need to pick a few of your pieces and get them to me. It's just a formality, so don't worry about it at all this week. Whatever you pick when you get back into town will be great, I'm sure. I know they'll be impressed."

Renee began planning immediately. Patty's voice cut through her thoughts. "Next week, Renee. You don't

need to work on it right now. I just knew you would
want to know."

She thanked Patty and hung up. She was still standing in the same spot she'd been when she had picked up
the phone, but now she dropped onto the bed.

It was actually happening. She couldn't believe it.

Despite Patty's parting words, Renee knew it would
be impossible for her to wait the entire week to get
started. She would need to go through each of her best
pieces and check them for any problems, then choose
which ones to submit.

An idea popped into her head, making her fingers
itch for her laptop. She could take Jessica's article and
design an amazing page around it, with the picture of
the barn front and center.

She knew it would be impressive and show off her
skills, but it would take time. She would need to get
started on it immediately.

It was MIDAFTERNOON when Jeremiah and Aaron pulled
up to Aaron's house. It had been a long day, and Jeremiah could barely contain his excitement as he walked
into the house. This was it. He and Renee would finally
get some time alone.

"I've got an idea," he said to his friend, as if the
thought had just sprung to mind. "How about I take
Renee out to town for dinner and some sightseeing?
That way you and Jessica can have some time alone
together. It must be weird having someone else around
all the time."

Aaron smiled and narrowed his eyes at Jeremiah,

giving him a sly look. "Are you trying to get together with Renee?"

Jeremiah laughed like the idea was crazy. He'd been prepared for this. "I just know how depraved you two are. It must be killing you not to grope each other every ten minutes."

Aaron nodded. "You have no idea."

"So I'm a great friend. Remember that." If things went the way Jeremiah hoped, he'd need all the brownie points he could muster.

With that, Jeremiah waltzed out of the room, ready to find Renee and get out of that house. A few hours alone, then a nice dinner together—maybe he could convince her that they had a future after all.

She was sitting on the living room couch, hunched over her laptop. He paused for a moment and just stared at her. His heart sped up as he imagined what her face would look like when he did all the things he wanted to do to her.

He walked up behind her and placed a hand on her shoulder. Even that much contact made his body react. She looked up, and the flush on her cheeks made it clear that she felt it, too. He couldn't wait another minute to kiss her. "We've been paroled. Let's go," he said in a whisper, gesturing toward the door.

She hesitated, looking back at her computer, and he knew something was wrong. "I'm kind of in the middle of something important. Give me a few minutes."

His good mood dampened. She hadn't seemed very happy about the idea of being alone with him, and the thought stabbed at him. He tried to put that thought out of his mind. It must be something else that was making her act like that. "Work?" he asked.

She nodded, staring at the screen. "My boss called this morning. They're going to offer me the job, but I need to send them a few of my page designs."

"And they're making you work on it while you're on vacation?" He felt annoyance on her behalf.

She looked at him. "Well, no, but I had an idea and wanted to get started on it."

"So, there's no good reason for you to be working on this right now? You're joking, right?"

He knew it came out harsher than he'd wanted, but he couldn't believe that she was putting off what they'd both been looking forward to for this. The thought that she wasn't as excited as he was only made his mood darker.

He could see her jaw working and knew she was frustrated. Hell, so was he. She shut her laptop with a snap and stood, but it was clear this wasn't over. Instead of walking over to him, she turned to leave the room, heading toward the stairs. "This is important to me," she threw back at him as she disappeared.

And I'm not, he thought, filling in the implied meaning.

Jeremiah wasn't sure if he wanted to storm out or race after her. Instead, he stood there, still looking at the door she'd disappeared through, until he heard a door upstairs close. Without another word, he left.

RENEE STOOD IN her room, trying to figure out what the hell had just happened. Why had Jeremiah acted like that?

She asked herself the question, but she knew the answer. The real question was, why had she hesitated? She'd been looking forward to this opportunity, and when it finally came, she'd stalled. What was she so afraid of?

Renee sat down on the bed and put her head in her hands. When he touched her on the shoulder, it was warm and sweet, and looking up at him made her heart light on fire and melt at the same time. It was the melting that had scared her enough to put off her chance to go with him.

But there was no reason to worry about falling for this guy. He certainly wouldn't be falling for her, and anyway, it was only one week. Then she'd be heading back to New York. Did she really want to go back without having any of the fun she'd promised herself?

God, she was an idiot. She stood and raced out of the room and down the stairs, not letting herself think too much about what she would do or say.

But it wouldn't have mattered anyway. She got to the door just in time to see his truck disappear.

She trudged back upstairs, to her laptop and pages. They suddenly didn't seem quite so interesting or important.

JEREMIAH MADE A circuit of the outside of his house, thinking. He felt like an idiot, and a meandering drive after leaving Jessica and Aaron's hadn't helped at all. He should never have imagined that he and Renee could be more than a short-term thing. He'd known from the beginning that she didn't want anything more than a casual fun week. She was a workaholic who refused to let anything more serious happen; she'd made that clear right off the bat.

So why had he let that fact get him so frustrated?

He sat on the stairs of the porch and looked up at the darkening sky. He'd let himself believe that maybe he could change that about her, but that was ridiculous. You can't change someone after just a few days of kisses and conversation.

No, he needed to accept that if he was going to have any type of relationship with Renee, it wasn't going to be anything more than her indulging a few fantasies. She wouldn't let her heart get involved.

That was what he'd agreed to, and if that was all he could get from her, so be it. Without ever entering the house, he got back into his truck. He needed to go apologize and see if he could salvage this thing.

By the time he got to Jessica and Aaron's, stars were dotting the sky above him. He walked in and found the two of them sitting at the kitchen table, the remnants of dinner still in front of them. Aaron looked up at him. "Hey, what happened?"

Jeremiah wasn't sure how to answer. In addition to making a mess of things with Renee, he hadn't exactly given his friend the privacy he'd promised. "Renee was working on something for her job," he answered with a shrug.

Jessica said, "She just came down for a second when I called her for dinner. Didn't even eat. She just said she was working. She didn't look good. Do you think she's sick?"

Jeremiah shrugged again, feeling guilty. Had he made her feel that bad? He was such an ass.

Aaron stood and grabbed a bottle of Johnnie Walker from the cupboard. "You don't look so good yourself. Here, have a drink."

Jeremiah couldn't really say no, and a drink sounded like a great idea. If Renee was that upset, giving her a little space was probably a good thing.

RENEE SAT ON her bed, staring at her computer screen. For over three hours, she'd been trying to work on her design, hoping she could lose herself in the clean lines of the page, but it wasn't working. Her mind wouldn't blank. It kept filling itself with Jeremiah, blocking out everything else, even work.

She looked at the clock. It wasn't even nine yet, but she was done with this day. She turned out the lights and lay down. The previous sleepless night caught up to her, and she was quickly asleep.

"SLOW DOWN, MAN. Is everything okay?"

Jeremiah looked at his empty glass. He hadn't meant to drink it all, but he'd been thinking about how he and Renee had left things and before he realized it, the whiskey was gone. He tried to decide what he could tell Aaron.

"I don't really want to get into details, but I'm trying to make things happen with a woman, and it's not quite working out the way I'd like."

Aaron leaned forward, interested. "What woman? Why is this the first I'm hearing about it?"

Jeremiah shook his head. "Not ready to talk about that, Aaron."

"Is she related to you or something?"

Jeremiah punched Aaron in the arm.

"Ow! What? It happens more than you think."

Jeremiah shook his head. "Anyway, she doesn't want anything serious."

Aaron raised his eyebrows. "And you do? Whoa. I didn't expect you to be ready to settle down."

Jeremiah didn't say anything else. He'd probably already said too much, but Aaron had been his best friend since kindergarten. It seemed weird to go through all this and leave him completely in the dark.

Aaron refilled their glasses. "Without knowing more, I can't really give you advice. But I say, if you think she's worth it, don't give up hope."

Jeremiah took another swallow of the brown liquid and thought about what Aaron had said. He'd never been the type to give up hope, so why would he start now? He wasn't sure if it was that thought or the alcohol, but he felt better.

Now he just needed to mend things with Renee.

"Is it okay if I stay the night?" he asked Aaron. "I don't want to drive home," he explained, gesturing at the empty glass and glad for the excuse.

Aaron nodded, and Jeremiah walked resolutely up the stairs, ready to patch things up with Renee. Thinking about spending time alone in her room made his body react immediately, but he tried to calm it back down.

Once he got to the top of the stairs, he paused and took a breath before knocking on the door to the left.

No answer.

He eased the door open. The room was dark and quiet, so he shut it again, disappointed. She was already asleep.

Jeremiah stood there for a long time, looking at Renee's door. He wanted to apologize, wanted more than anything to kiss her and finally do what they'd been edging toward since she arrived. But she had made it clear only a few hours ago that she was mad at him, so barging in, even to apologize, while she was sleeping when he was a little beyond tipsy, seemed like a terrible idea in so many ways.

He wanted to see her so badly, but even through the alcohol he was able to convince himself that it wasn't the best time. He finally turned to the door on the right, his usual room. He promised himself that he would talk to her in the morning, when she was awake and he was sober.

He went into his room, leaving the light off. Jeremiah pulled off his shoes and pants and dropped into bed before he could make any stupid decisions.

RENEE WOKE SLOWLY, not wanting to let go of the delicious feeling of Jeremiah's hard body spread out next to her like a yummy treat. She pressed her lips against his, opening in invitation. It was only as his tongue slid enticingly over her teeth that she realized she was no longer asleep.

This couldn't be real, could it?

She opened her eyes. The room was dark, but there was just enough light coming in through the window for her to see Jeremiah's outline beside her. "You're real," she said aloud before realizing how stupid it sounded.

"Real," he affirmed, before leaning in to kiss her again.

She wasn't sure when he'd sneaked into her room, or even what he was doing at Jessica and Aaron's house in the first place, but those questions fled from her mind as he kissed her even more deeply, groaning with the sensation of it.

She pressed herself against him, sinking into the kiss. Any worries or hesitation she had had before were gone. All that was left was her need to touch him everywhere. Her hands slid down his bare stomach until they reached his boxers and his erection.

He was definitely real. No question about it. She wrapped her fingers around him and squeezed.

He groaned again. "You're killing me, Renee."

She gave him a devilish grin he couldn't see. She hadn't even begun.

He leaned in to kiss her again, this time his breathing ragged and quick. His fingers clenched in her hair for a moment before starting a slow crawl down her body.

When his hand reached her breast, her already-speeding pulse increased, making her feel light-headed. Her nipples tightened into hard nubs at his touch, and the sensation was so intense she thought she might orgasm right then and there.

She pushed him flat on his back, and leaned over him, kissing his chest, tasting and teasing his skin as she moved downward, inching closer to his iron-hard erection. "Whoa, what are you doing?" Jeremiah asked, in a voice that said he knew exactly what she was doing.

He just wanted to hear her say it.

She smiled in the dark, pressing a small bite to his abs. "What I've been wanting to do since I saw you in Vegas."

With that, she slid down his boxers and took him into her mouth, relishing the taste of him.

He moaned again and throbbed against her lips. A feeling of power surged through her—this incredibly sexy man was totally under her control, and she reveled in it. After only a few moments, though, Jeremiah sat up, and before she was sure what happened, she was flat on her back. "I wasn't finished," she told him.

He chuckled. "If I let you keep going, I would be, and I don't want this to be over yet."

With that, his hands and lips went to work on her body, moving over every inch of her until she was so alive with sensation that she couldn't think.

He moved between her legs, his mouth and hand converging at her center. As his fingers curled inside her, he applied his tongue to her mound, sending her over the edge so sharply that she had to bite her hand to keep from screaming out. She shuddered as the spasms of sensation hurtled through her body.

She clenched and unclenched her hands, trying to bring herself back under control, but Jeremiah seemed to have no intention of allowing that. He bit her thigh, then soothed the spot with his tongue, continuing the pattern down one leg, then back up the other. His caresses only gave her a moment of respite before bringing her back to the cliff's edge. She couldn't wait any longer. "I want you in me," she said, hardly able to create a coherent sentence. "Now."

Jeremiah didn't need to be told twice, which was good because Renee had used the last of her ability to speak on that sentence. He leaned away from her, leaving only cool air in his wake. For a moment, she wanted to call him back to her, but then she heard the ripping of a condom wrapper. In a moment he was back with her, his hard, hot body against her, then on top of her. Finally he slid inside her, filling her. The sensation making her gasp.

She wrapped her legs around him, pulling him even deeper, and he groaned out her name, his voice deep and primal. They rocked together, breaths mingling as they kissed. As much as Renee had imagined and fantasized about it, she still couldn't believe what was happening. The incredibly sexy Jeremiah was ravishing her mouth with his tongue, while the rest of him moved in a slow rhythm building toward what she knew was the inevitable conclusion.

Slow curls of ecstasy wrapped through her as he began to move faster, and she lost herself in the sensations. He nipped at her earlobe and whispered her name, and she fell over the edge once more. He squeezed her hand in his as he followed.

8

JEREMIAH OPENED HIS EYES. The early-morning light streamed through the window, making Renee's hair blaze like a reddish-blond halo framing her face. She was so beautiful he wanted to run his hand over her cheek to be sure she was real, but resisted the urge. He didn't want to wake her up.

His mind replayed everything that had happened. He had thought sex with her would be great, but it was so much more. Incredible, that's what it was. Everything about her was amazing. The way her lips felt against his, the way she tasted, the little squeals she made as she came for him.

He wanted it all, over and over again.

As if she could read his thoughts, Renee snuggled closer to him, kissing his shoulder as she opened her eyes. "Good morning," she said with a nibble that shot through his heart and straight down to his groin.

"If you keep doing that," he said through his teeth as he struggled to maintain control, "I'm going to have to do things to you."

"Oh yeah?" she responded with a mischievous smirk. "What kind of things?"

"The kind that would probably come to Jessica and Aaron's attention."

Her groan of annoyance was so adorable that he chuckled, which turned quickly to a sharp intake of air as her fingers slid along his already-hard shaft. He pulled her hand away, cupping it in his own. "You should probably head back to your room before they wake up," he told her, wishing he was saying something very different.

Confusion swept across her features before being replaced by understanding. She sat up. "This is your room," she said.

Jeremiah was nonplussed. "Whose room did you think it was when you sneaked in here last night?"

Renee shook her head. "You don't understand. Jessica switched me into this room. *You* sneaked into *my* room. On accident, apparently."

She sounded deflated, and it took him a moment to figure out why. Then he realized and squeezed the hand he still held. "I tried to go to your room last night to apologize, but the light was off and I didn't want to wake you up." He laughed. "Apparently I was being polite to an empty room."

Her mood brightened immediately, and his heart thumped harder in his chest. "So, I guess I should go back to my room, which isn't my room?" he asked, a little confused.

She nodded, but the regret on her face was too much for him. He wished he didn't have to go, but then he had an idea. He sat up beside her and kissed her and in seconds they were both breathless. "Throw on some clothes," he told her.

She looked so disappointed he didn't know if he should laugh or hug her close. "I have a plan. It's a good one, trust me."

The disappointment was replaced with curiosity, but he shook his head before she had the chance to ask. "Just put on some clothes. I'm going to the other room for a minute. I'll meet you at the bottom of the stairs, okay?"

He tossed on his clothes and opened the door carefully, trying to keep it from squeaking. As soon as he was sure the coast was clear, he hastened across the hall to what he had believed to be Renee's room. After a few seconds making the bed look slept-in, he was back in the hallway and bounding down the stairs as quietly as he could. He was filled with a nervous excitement as he assured himself that the house was still quiet, its owners still asleep.

Renee came down the stairs only a minute after him. He raised a finger to his lips to let her know to be quiet, then grabbed her hand and pulled her after him out the door. He didn't need to hold her hand for this part, but it just felt so good. They began walking down the property, the barn ahead and slightly to the right of them.

Once they were outside, she asked, "Where are we going?"

"To see the river that runs along through the trees."

"Maybe I should have grabbed a coat," she said, rubbing the goose bumps on her arms.

The cool morning breeze swept over them and she

shivered. He wrapped his arm around her and pulled her close. They began to pass the barn. "The river is silvery with tiny waterfalls. It babbles and everything."

"It sounds nice," she responded, clearly still wondering what he had in mind.

"What does the river look like?" he asked her as they passed behind the barn.

Her forehead wrinkled. He waited, and after a beat she answered, "Silver with little waterfalls?"

"Perfect," he said, then stopped walking. "Now you know how to answer if Jessica or Aaron asks you about it."

With that, he opened a small door in the back of the barn and gestured for her to follow. Renee's confusion changed to delight as his plan became clear, and she walked quickly to catch up to him.

In no time, they had made their way through the building and up to the loft. The excitement in Jeremiah's stomach was reaching a fever pitch. The moment they were hidden away in the hay-scented loft—either as an added protection against discovery, or because it seemed really sexy—Jeremiah pulled Renee toward him and gave her the long kiss he'd been waiting for all morning.

In moments, Jeremiah's blood was pounding in his veins, and his erection was straining the zipper of his jeans. His hands roved over Renee's body, enjoying every piece of her they could find. He leaned back for a second to get a full view of her face. Her lips were swollen from the kiss, her hair disheveled, and she wasn't wearing any makeup. She was the most beautiful woman he'd ever seen.

He moved back toward her and kissed her again. This was the best morning of his life, hands down.

RENEE PUT HER hand on Jeremiah's chest and grabbed a fistful of his shirt, as if hanging on for dear life. Which, in a way, she was. Last night had proven that her fantasies hadn't even come close to the real deal. Her knees were still weak from those bone-shattering orgasms, and here she was moving quickly toward another one. With Jeremiah's arm wrapped around her, holding her up, who needed knees?

Jeremiah's lips and tongue and teeth moved down her neck, leaving a wet trail that sizzled with heat. As he moved lower, he said, "You told me you fantasized about us getting together. What exactly did you imagine us doing?"

With another guy, Renee would feel embarrassed about describing her fantasies, but with Jeremiah there was just the thrill of knowing that whatever she said, he would be an incredibly willing participant. "I pictured myself on top of you, riding you until I came."

Jeremiah stilled for a second and the breath whooshed out of him. "Good fantasy," he murmured against her ear.

And then he got to work undressing them both. Renee's hand was no longer holding a fistful of his shirt, but instead lay flat against his chest, feeling the warm, taut skin stretched over muscles that would make any woman melt.

She pressed her hand against him, directing him to lie down on the floor of the loft. His eyes were dark with arousal, and his cock stood straight at attention as she unrolled the condom along his length.

She kissed his chest as she positioned herself on top of him, straddling him. He groaned. "Really, *really* good fantasy."

When she took him inside her, a small scream escaped her at the pleasure of it. Every glorious inch of him filled her. She began to move, the friction where their bodies joined making her entire being feel tight and sensitive. Then his thumb moved between her legs, sliding against her nub until she cried out again.

He touched and teased her as she rode him, his head thrown back and every muscle taut. She moved faster, rushing toward release. It exploded through her, making every part of her quiver, and he came with her, gasping her name.

She leaned forward, her body on top of his, feeling deliciously spent. His skin smelled of sweat and sex, and she breathed it deep into her lungs, enjoying it. His arms slid around her, holding her close.

Renee opened her eyes, suddenly uncomfortable. It felt more like a love scene than she liked. It was just sex. Really good sex, but that was it. She couldn't let it turn into anything more than that or she'd be nursing a broken heart when she went back to New York. There was no other way for that path to end.

Jeremiah shifted slightly to look at her face. "Hey, you okay?" he asked, concern in his voice.

She sat up and slid off him, hating how empty she

felt when he was no longer inside her. She forced herself to be perky and pleasant. "Yep, I'm fine. Do you think Jessica and Aaron will be up?"

He looked like he wanted to ask something else, but to her relief he just shrugged. "Probably."

She stood and started getting into her clothes. "Good, because I'm starving and the only breakfast food I'm capable of making is toast." She cringed at her own fake tones.

"Don't knock toast. It's the key to a great breakfast," he answered, giving her his lighthearted smile.

She tried to ignore the fact that only his mouth smiled. His eyes still held concern.

Renee turned to the ladder, trying to get away from those eyes. "I only burn it like sixty percent of the time."

Once she was at the bottom of the ladder, she brushed herself off one last time, feeling anxious in Jeremiah's presence, though she wasn't completely sure why. When he was standing beside her, she turned for inspection, more to mask her discomfort than anything else. "Is there any hay or anything on me? I don't want to leave any clues for Jessica to pick up on."

Jeremiah took a step closer, halting her nervous movements. The deep brown of his eyes sucked her in, calming her jitters. "Would it really be the worst thing in the world if Jessica found out?" he asked her.

She knew he wasn't asking just that question. He was asking another one, a question that sent the panic monster running through her brain. She turned her eyes away from his, breaking away from that intoxicating stare. It was time to make this completely clear for both of them. "Yes. If Jessica knew what was going on, she would either be horrified that her little sister was having a fling instead of helping her with the wedding, or she would get excited and think that this is going to turn into something more, which it won't."

She paused for a second, letting her words sink in. She still couldn't look at him. "Since it can't go beyond this week, Jessica absolutely can't find out."

For what felt like a very long time, neither of them spoke. Then he began walking toward the barn door. "Rules one and two—Jessica can't know, and this is just for the week. Got it."

She followed him as he walked in silence back to the house. Renee wanted to bring back the fun, easygoing banter she so enjoyed with him, but couldn't think of anything else to say.

When she was lying there with him, it didn't feel like a simple fling—it felt more serious than that. And that was exactly what she *didn't* want. She just needed to get back to fun and flirty, and nothing else. Once she figured out how to break through this awkwardness.

As soon as they were inside the house, the sounds and smells of breakfast bombarded her senses. Aaron was at the stove again in his garish apron.

"That thing looks ridiculous on you. You know that, right?" Jeremiah said as he sat down.

"Well, good morning to you, too. I like this apron. Best present you ever gave me."

"What about that football I got you that was signed by the entire 1995 Dallas Cowboys team?"

Aaron's eyes shifted. "That...kind of exploded."

"What!"

"I hooked it up to the electric pump to inflate it a little bit, but you look away for one second—apparently there's a limit to how much air it'll hold."

Jeremiah seemed suspicious. "One second, huh? Was Jessica in the room?"

Aaron answered with a grin. Jeremiah shook his head. "You win. From now on, I'm not getting you anything but girlie kitchen items."

"Great! I need pot holders."

Jeremiah glanced at Renee and smiled. A real, genuine smile that she couldn't help but return.

She sat down next to him, stifling a laugh, either of amusement at the boys' conversation or relief that the unease between her and Jeremiah was gone. This was the Jeremiah she wanted, not the sweet, caring one who made her heart ache in a way that bothered her.

Jessica walked into the kitchen. "Good morning. What have you two been up to?"

Renee tried to keep her face from betraying her. "We went for a walk to the river."

Jessica's eyes lit up. "Isn't it beautiful?"

"I love the little waterfalls," Renee responded, seeing Jeremiah's grin out of the corner of her eye and almost breaking character.

Jessica seemed satisfied and shifted her attention to Jeremiah. "Sorry I gave away your room without telling you. Aaron and I didn't realize how weird that must have been for you until this morning. I hope it didn't cause any problems last night."

Renee purposely avoided looking at Jeremiah, but

she knew exactly what he was thinking. *It caused a lot of very good things*. He just said, "No problem," and they moved on without getting any closer to that land mine.

Aaron served up another amazing breakfast and Jessica began discussing the tasks for the day, including setting up the chairs in the barn.

"If you need to work," Jeremiah said, turning to her, "I can help out setting stuff up."

It was such a sweet gesture, and he was so clearly apologizing for the day before that she was halfway to a puddle of goo before she managed to get a hold of herself.

She certainly had a lot to do if she wanted to get that spread perfect before the end of the week, but she'd come all this way to help her sister. Thoughts warred inside her.

Finally, she decided on a compromise. "How about we both set up the chairs? Everything will get done faster, and *then* I can do some work before…"

Before what? Before they spent another night together? God, she hoped so.

His lips twitched at the corners and he nodded.

"It's settled," Jessica said, her voice slicing the moment to shreds. "Let's eat, clean up, and then we can all get to work."

They ate and made conversation, but Renee missed pretty much all of it. She was far too intent upon Jeremiah's hand, which pressed lightly against her thigh under the table. It wasn't much, definitely not something that would catch the attention of the other two, but oh man, it caught hers.

By the time breakfast was over, she could feel her eyes glazing over, and she was little more than a puddle. How could he do so much to her with just the backs of his fingers under the table?

Unfortunately, there was no time to explore the question in more detail. Jessica was already divvying up tasks. "I need a quick shower," Renee said before Jessica could give her another job. After the night before and then the romp in the loft, she felt like she was exuding sex out of her pores, and any moment, Jessica was going to catch on.

Jessica nodded. "You do that while we wash the dishes."

Renee stood, a little shaky on legs made of jelly. Jeremiah shifted uncomfortably before standing, and Renee laughed quietly under her breath. Apparently his little bit of below-the-table teasing had tortured him as much as her.

Renee didn't realize her sister was standing next to her until she spoke, startling her. "What's funny?" Jessica asked.

Renee couldn't think of a thing to say. Her mind was blank.

JEREMIAH SAW RENEE's panic and thought of something as fast as he could. "You were thinking about that terrible joke I told you on the walk back, weren't you?" he said.

Both women turned to him.

"What's the joke?" Aaron asked, picking up the dishes.

"Okay, but prepare yourself. It's pretty bad," Jeremiah said, turning on his "joker" setting to full blast to get the attention off Renee. "Did you hear about the circus fire? It was intense."

There was a silent pause.

"Get it? *In. Tents.* A circus fire."

Jessica nodded. "You're right. That's a horrible joke."

The moment was over, and Jessica and Aaron started to turn back to cleaning off the table. Renee, however, was still staring at him. As he watched, her silent giggles turned into loud guffaws. She was laughing so hard she looked like she could barely breathe. His heart seemed to leap in his chest as he watched her, blown away by how adorable she was.

When she finally got control of herself and moved to leave the room, she sent him one last look, and it sizzled across the space between them. They were both thinking the same thing, he was sure, but Jessica and Aaron would *definitely* notice something was up if he went with her into the shower.

So instead he would stay downstairs and wait until she appeared again, driving himself crazy with the image of her soapy and wet with water running down her silky skin. It seemed like the only thing to do.

RENEE LEANED FORWARD until her head was fully under the hot streaming water and she let it run over her. She hated to admit to herself how much she wanted Jeremiah there with her, and not just for his sexy body.

That was one reason, certainly, but not the only one.

She wanted to talk to him more, just to hear what he would say. And that was a problem she would need to get over.

In a week-long one-night stand, it seemed better not to love the guy's personality. That just made things harder when the week ended.

She finished rinsing and turned off the water. Once she was dry and dressed, she went downstairs, where the rest of the group sat at the table. The look in Jeremiah's eyes as she stepped into the kitchen made a zing of electricity shoot through her. Instead of being satiated by that recent sexcapade and rocking orgasm, she was ready to curl her legs around his body and take him for another ride.

That just wasn't in the cards for the moment, though. Jessica was already up and ushering them out of the house, and there was no choice but to follow.

As they all trouped out to the barn, Jeremiah sidled up beside her and slowed down, allowing Aaron and Jessica to get ahead of them. The air crackled between them, shooting sparks of desire through her. There was so much Renee wanted to say, but the only words that formulated in her brain were: *I want you so badly right now*. And that wouldn't help either of them get through these next few hours.

"Thanks for saving my ass back there. And nice joke," Renee told him under her breath instead.

She clasped one hand in the other to keep from reaching out and touching him. Jessica might not be the most observant person, but she'd probably notice if Renee started groping the best man.

"Glad you liked it," he answered quietly. "I've been saving it to tell you. That seemed like a good time."

His fingers brushed hers for just a second, sending another jolt through her, and then he sped up to help Aaron push aside the heavy barn door. She took in a deep breath, trying to keep the bones in her body where they were instead of turning to mush and melting into a pool of desire.

Just as she had the time before, Renee stopped to watch as the two men rolled open the large door to the picturesque barn. Her mind managed to focus on the scene in front of her, and immediately the gears in her head began to turn.

"Jessica, you have a decent camera, right?" she called to her sister.

Jessica looked confused about the seemingly random question, but nodded. Renee ran up and grabbed her hand, pulling her back toward the house. "I need it."

"Now?"

"Now." Renee turned to the men, who had just gotten the door fully open. "Shut the door again, guys. I need to get a picture of you opening it."

She didn't wait for a response. Her mind was buzzing too fast to slow down as she hustled Jessica back inside. The sunlight, the barn, the men. It was all perfect, and she needed that photo to grace Jessica's story and her page design. But she had to move quickly if she wanted to capture that magic.

In no time, she had the camera around her neck and was running back down toward the barn. "Open the door slowly," she commanded to Aaron and Jeremiah, raising the camera to her face.

The shutter clicked again and again as the barn door opened, and once it was in place, the two men turned to Renee. "What was that all about?" Aaron asked.

"Something for work," Renee mumbled, not looking at him, her thoughts occupied.

She stared intently at the screen on the back of the camera, reviewing the photos she'd captured. There. Renee couldn't help the grin that spread across her face. She had found the perfect one for her page.

Giddy, she turned to Jessica. "This photo will look perfect with your article."

Jessica narrowed her eyes at her sister, but then she looked down at the screen and her expression changed. "Wow. That's an amazing picture."

Renee noted that Jessica hadn't said anything about *not* using the article. Could this day get any better?

She took the camera back to the house, holding it carefully, as if it was a priceless treasure.

Renee set the camera on her bed. She was itching to sit down and work on the spread, but everyone was expecting her to return to the barn and the business of wedding preparations.

At least in the barn she'd be able to watch Jeremiah. Her lips curled into a smile as she thought about the muscles in his arms rippling as he moved heavy objects. Maybe she'd even get lucky and he would need to bend over to work on something, giving her a great view of his ass.

That thought sent her bounding down the stairs and

to the door. Before she could open it, though, Jeremiah stepped through, and his lips were on hers.

Renee had no idea why he was there or if Jessica would be following right behind him, but she couldn't care too much when Jeremiah was kissing her like that.

Just as the kiss began to deepen and her fingers crept along the waistband of his jeans, he stepped away from her, leaving her kissing nothing but air.

"We'd better get back," he said. "Jessica forgot her wedding notebook and I volunteered to grab it for her, but if I take too long, she might get suspicious and come looking."

Renee nodded and started for the door, but before she could reach it, Jeremiah grabbed her arm and pulled her in for one last kiss. This time, she was the one who pulled away, though reluctantly. "The notebook, remember?"

He gave her his sexy sideways grin. "Couldn't help myself. I'll see you out there."

She left him to search for the notebook and headed back to the barn, heady from the kiss.

This day was definitely in the running for the best day of her life.

9

JEREMIAH MOVED ANOTHER chair into place as per Jessica's instructions, and went to grab a few more. Renee was a couple of rows ahead of him with Jessica, adjusting the angle so the seated guests would all be facing the altar area at the far end of the barn. Her strawberry blond hair fell in her face in a way that sent a delightful pang through his heart.

He had it bad, there was no denying it. What kind of trouble was he getting himself into?

Once they were all working as per Jessica's instructions, she disappeared inside to double-check something while the rest of them continued with the barn. Jeremiah hoped Aaron would leave as well and give him some time with Renee, but no such luck.

When they were finished, Aaron said, "I'm heading back to the house. You two coming?"

Finally, Jeremiah thought.

"I want to adjust a few of these rows first," Renee said immediately.

"I'll help. We'll meet you up there in a few minutes," Jeremiah added.

The moment Aaron was gone they headed for each other. A couple of minutes was all they had, but they took advantage of it.

Renee was in Jeremiah's arms immediately, and the carnal passion of her kiss sent fire through his veins and straight to his groin. When her tongue slipped past his teeth, it was all he could do not to pull her to the ground and take her right there.

"We'd better go in," Renee said when they broke apart, much too soon for Jeremiah's taste.

"I'm right behind you," he said, trying to bring himself back under control.

He watched her walk toward the house, a now-familiar pain in his heart.

RENEE WALKED INTO the house and almost tripped over a suitcase. Her suitcase. Before she could formulate any thoughts beyond the oddity of her suitcase being in front of the door, Jessica was walking into the room with her phone to her ear. She didn't look happy.

"We'll see you tomorrow then. And you're sure it'll be dry by Thursday?"

She nodded to herself, thanked whoever she was talking to, and hung up with a sigh. Renee was still standing in the doorway, utterly confused.

Jessica looked at her sister with an exasperated smile. "You know how something always manages to go wrong?" she asked.

Renee walked over to her sister, preparing herself to

deal with a Jessica freak-out. *Wrong* was one of her sister's least favorite words. "What happened?"

"A pipe burst upstairs while we were out in the barn. The carpet in the guest rooms is completely soaked."

Renee's eyes grew wide. Jessica just shrugged, and Renee wondered if she'd actually heard her sister correctly. How could she be so calm? "You're handling this really well," she said.

"I panicked at first, but a plumber's on his way, and I just got off the phone with a carpet cleaning company. They'll be coming by tomorrow, and they promised everything will be dry and ready by the time people start arriving on Thursday. It's all under control."

Renee's suitcase suddenly made sense. "My room—"

"Flooded," Jessica finished.

Renee nodded. "I'll just get a hotel room for a few days. No big deal."

Jessica shook her head. "You don't need to do that. I'm sure Jeremiah will help us out and take you in for a couple days. If that's okay with you."

Renee's heart started to pound so hard it hurt, and she felt like jumping in the air. A couple of days—and nights—at Jeremiah's? Yes, please.

She forced herself to nod calmly. "That's fine."

Her inner self was dancing a jig, and it seemed like every inch of her was revving up for what surely lay ahead. *Lay* being the operative word.

Was it too soon to leave?

Apparently not, as Jeremiah walked in the door and placed his hand on the top of her suitcase. He acted casual, but his eyes were gleaming with a fire that heated her entire body. "Did Jessica tell you about the pipe?" he asked.

She nodded.

"Are you okay staying with me for a couple of days?"

She wanted to laugh at the hesitation in his voice. She wanted to fist pump the air and have an impromptu dance scene like in a Bollywood film.

She nodded again.

He smiled. "Great. I'll get your suitcase in the truck. We can leave whenever you're ready."

Oh, she was ready.

Jessica gave her a quick hug. "Thanks for being so good about this. You two can come over tomorrow if you want, but we'll be able to get along fine without you if you want to explore the town or something. Thursday will be a busy day, though."

Renee's brain was only capturing words in fits and starts, but she understood the gist. Sex all day tomorrow.

After reassuring herself that her sister really wasn't freaking out over the carpets, Renee followed Jeremiah out to his truck and hopped in. Hell, she practically flew in. Jeremiah got behind the wheel, and then they were on their way to his house and complete freedom.

Neither spoke at first, but the grin on Jeremiah's face spoke volumes. Renee clasped her hands in her lap, trying to keep them off Jeremiah until they were at his house. It took only a mile for her to fail in that attempt, and she unbuckled her seat belt, slid over on the bench seat and buckled into the middle seat, tucking her body close to Jeremiah's.

She saw his jaw tighten, and a rush of desire enveloped her. He was attempting desperately to hold himself together, but he was going to break if she had anything to say about it. She ran her hand along his leg, from his knee up to his thigh, then up a little farther.

"We're never going to make it the five minutes to my house if you keep doing that," he told her through his clenched teeth.

"Maybe I don't want to wait that long."

Renee had spent enough time on their first ride imagining them having sex in his truck that she was pretty sure they could make it work just fine. And she was certainly willing to try it. Leaning over to nibble on his ear, she said, "Five minutes seems like a very long time."

He growled in agreement, and the truck bounced slightly as he pulled it off the road and behind a small copse of trees. Before she had time to react, the engine was off, as were their seat belts, and she was engulfed by his scent and warmth as his arms wrapped around her, pulling her onto his lap.

She found herself settled between him and the steering wheel, his lips and tongue drawing a line of fire along her collarbone as his hands danced around her breasts, turning her nipples into hard buttons of sensation. Feeling his hard hot erection pressed against her leg made her pulse jump, and her heart pounded so hard in her chest that she might have been worried if she'd had the ability to think.

She leaned back against the wheel, giving him more access, and he took advantage of it. Her bra was unhooked in seconds, and her shirt was lifted, exposing her chest to his ministrations. His tongue swirled around the areola of first one breast, then the other, and then he took each of her nipples into his mouth in turn.

She pressed herself back into the steering wheel harder. It took several seconds and Jeremiah's anguished movements away from her chest before she realized she was leaning on the horn.

JEREMIAH GROANED. WHAT the hell was he doing? Had he really been planning on them having sex right here, in this very not-secluded spot fifteen feet from the highway? The loud insistent horn was just the icing on the cake to ensure that they would be caught.

As delicious as Renee was, he forced himself to stop. He wanted her naked, but he would need to wait the few minutes until they reached his house. It was definitely a view he wanted to keep all to himself.

Renee slid off his lap onto the seat beside him, then moved back to her original spot, leaving the middle seat open between them. Jeremiah knew he should be happy for the brain-clearing space, but all he wanted was to pull her back on his lap. Not touching her seemed like an impossible challenge.

He fumbled with the key, trying to get the engine to start, but all his attention was on her. With her hair and clothes disheveled, her skin tinged with pink, as if she was very warm, she looked so sexy that he couldn't pull his eyes away.

It was only when she looked at him with that fire in her eyes and in a husky whisper told him, "Your place. Now," that he managed to turn to the task at hand.

With herculean effort, he got the truck started and

back on the road. Neither of them spoke, but their heavy breathing filled the cabin with barely controlled desire.

When they were almost at his ranch, he had himself under control enough to glance at Renee again out of the corner of his eye. She had put herself mostly to rights, but her parted lips and lowered eyelids gave away the fact that she hadn't managed to calm down completely.

Perfect.

He forced himself not to speed too much the last mile, and then they were parked beside his house. The moment the engine died, Renee was back on his lap, by his efforts or hers, he couldn't be sure.

He kissed her, plundering her mouth and sending his body into a frenzy. He managed somehow to get the truck door open, and without removing his lips from hers, he held her tight to his body and got them both out of the truck.

Once they were on solid ground, Renee straightened up and stood beside him. "You can show me your place later," she said, breathless, as she pulled him toward the door.

He fumbled with his keys in his haste to get the door open, but somehow he managed it, and then they were inside. The moment the door shut behind them, Renee was back in his arms, her body pressed against him, making him groan deep in his throat. God, she was sexy.

She pulled her shirt over her head, and he ran his hands over her creamy smooth skin. She shivered at his touch. Another shot of heat went straight through his heart and down to his cock, pushing the zipper of his pants to its limits.

Renee slipped off her bra, exposing her luscious breasts, her erect nipples. He leaned over to suck one into his mouth, satisfaction coursing through him as she gasped. He wanted to give her the time of her life. "Tell me another one of your fantasies."

She was silent for a minute, as if she was thinking. He moved to her other breast, swirling his tongue around the pert nipple before bringing it into his mouth, his teeth scraping lightly against her skin, earning him another gasp, this time turning into a moan that he felt through to his core. "Cowboy hat," she managed.

He had to smile. "The New York City girl has a thing for cowboys, huh?"

"Not until I saw you," she said.

He liked this woman. Every second that he passed in her presence made him more and more sure that he wanted to be with her beyond just this week.

He pushed that thought away. For now, he was just going to enjoy the present, and he was going to make sure she enjoyed it, too. He pushed her gently onto the couch and opened the coat closet near the door, grabbing his cowboy hat from the shelf. "No shirt!" she called out from her spot on the couch, making him chuckle.

"Yes ma'am," he said in his most twangy cowboy accent.

As per instructions, he took off his shirt and placed the hat on his head. When he turned around, he gave her his most smoldering smile, tilted his hat to her, and said, "Howdy."

He'd never actually said "howdy" to anyone before in his life, and the moment he said it he realized how stupid it sounded. She laughed, and so did he. He took off the hat. "Didn't really pull that off, did I?"

She shook her head. "Nope. How can you be so bad at acting like a cowboy? You *are* a cowboy."

"I've been so busy taking care of horses and other actual cowboy things that I forgot to take lessons on how to say 'howdy' just like they do in the movies. I never learned how to spit tobacco juice, either."

Renee grimaced at the idea of airborne tobacco liquid. His heart thumped. How did she manage to make a grimace cute? Man, he had it bad for this woman. "Okay, no fake cowboy talk. I can still pull off the hat, though. After all, this is my actual hat, so I should be able to make it seem real."

He put the hat on his head again, tipped forward, and then pushed it up with one index finger so it slid backward. Fire danced in Renee's eyes, and she exhaled slowly, nodding. She didn't say anything, but she didn't have to.

Walking over to her, he noted how her eyes roved over his entire body. He wanted to move faster, so it could be her hands instead of just her eyes that were doing the touching, but if this was one of her fantasies, he wanted to do it right.

When he reached where she was sitting on the couch, he dropped to his knees in front of her. She spread her jean-clad legs farther apart to allow room for him, and he put one hand on each of her legs. As his hands slid along the fabric toward her thighs, he could feel her body tensing with excitement.

His hands kept going until they reached where the material joined, and one hand rubbed over the area, creating pressure on the sensitive skin beneath. When she leaned back at his touch, spreading her legs wider for him, the pressure in his own jeans reached a new capacity he would've imagined to be impossible.

He kept rubbing, reveling in her pleasure, and his gaze slid from the damp spot on her jeans that showed exactly how excited she was up along her smooth stomach, lingering on the luscious peaks of her breasts, and finally landing on her entrancing face. Her head was tilted back against the couch cushions, her lips slightly parted. Her eyes were open and looking down at him, watching what he was doing.

His whole body tightened as he looked at her. He took the hat off his head and placed it on hers, then leaned forward and began kissing, biting and licking the silky skin of her stomach that he'd admired moments before. He pressed in closer, spreading her legs even wider and giving his mouth access to her pert breasts, teasing the already-hard nipples with his tongue until Renee's breathing turned ragged.

He kept going, touching and licking until her body shook as an orgasm washed through her. She cried out with the force of it, and his dick jumped so hard at the sound that he would have worried about the zipper of his pants if he'd been able to think of anything but Renee.

As she came back to Earth, he leaned back slightly to get a better view of her face beneath the cowboy hat.

Her eyes were closed, all the muscles of her face relaxed. "Was that what you had in mind?" he asked her.

She began to nod, then opened her eyes and smirked at him from beneath the brim of his hat. "Well, it was a good start, but the fantasy isn't over yet."

With that, she pushed lightly on his chest until he was resting on his haunches. Then she undid her jeans and slipped them off, revealing lacy black panties and shapely legs. When she took the panties off, too, he could hardly control himself, but he stayed still, watching to see what she would do next.

She planted her legs on either side of him once again, opening herself fully to his view and making his heart pump so forcefully that one part of his mind wondered vaguely if he might have a heart attack. If he did, it definitely wasn't the worst way to go.

Renee leaned forward and hooked a finger into one of the belt loops of his pants and tugged him back onto his knees in the space between her legs. She stopped tugging, but he kept moving forward, placing one of those smooth bare limbs over his shoulder as he leaned in to taste her.

As his mouth slid over her sex, she moaned his name. Fire shot through his veins. "Dammit, Jeremiah," she said in a husky voice, "I was trying to be the one in charge, and now I can barely move."

"Do you want me to stop?" he asked, moving back slightly.

"God, no."

He chuckled and leaned forward again. His tongue flicked her clitoris until he knew she was almost at the edge of another orgasm, and then he slipped a finger inside her. She gasped out, "You. Inside."

He couldn't have made a coherent sentence at that moment, either. He unzipped his jeans and finally let his throbbing erection free. As he slipped on a condom, she took the hat off her head and put it back on his.

Before he could change positions, she looped her hands around his neck and pulled him toward her, and then her lips were on his, kissing him as if her life depended on it. She wrapped her legs around him, and still crouching in front of the couch, he entered her. She groaned deep in her throat, but didn't break off the kiss.

He sank into her warmth, then pulled almost entirely out, then back in. As he started a rhythmic motion, she copied it with her tongue inside his mouth. It drove him wild, and he moved faster and faster until they were hanging on to each other, gasping with the intensity of the moment. And then she was gone, crying out his name as she climaxed, and he followed.

Once Jeremiah had slightly regained the ability to think, he tightened an arm around Renee's waist and shifted until he was on the couch with her on top of him, her weight settled on his chest. He wasn't quite ready to slide out of her yet. It felt so good to be with her like this. So *right*.

She lifted her head and gave him a contented smile. He wondered if she felt it too, but he wasn't ready to ask. Not yet.

Instead, he said, "I need a shower. How about you?"

"A shower sounds fantastic," she replied.

They left their clothes in a disorderly heap on the living room floor, forgotten.

RENEE WOKE UP SLOWLY, enjoying the pleasant ache in her body from so much physical activity. The night before replayed in her mind and she smiled with her eyes still closed. Then her stomach grumbled and she realized she was starving.

She was more than glad to be out from under Jessica's watchful eye, but dammit if she couldn't use one of Aaron's epic breakfasts.

She finally opened her eyes and saw that she was alone in bed. Where was Jeremiah?

As Renee got out of bed to search for him—and hopefully find food along the way—she remembered that all her clothes except what she had worn yesterday were in her suitcase, which was still in the back of Jeremiah's truck. And the clothes she was wearing had never made it off the living room floor.

In her relaxed state, jeans seemed way too much hassle even if they were easy to find.

A quick glance around, though, and she discovered that her jeans actually were very easy to find. All her clothes, in fact. They'd been folded and placed on an overstuffed chair in the corner of the room, beside a clean pair of men's pajamas.

Her heart started to melt before she reminded it that this was a fun fling and there was to be no heart melting involved. It was a nice gesture, sure, but not something to get all gooey about.

Just to prove that this was all supposed to be sexy

and not real life, she left the pajama pants on the chair and only put on the shirt. It was long enough to cover her, but not by much.

Then she went off in search of Jeremiah.

The moment she opened the bedroom door, she could hear music playing somewhere in the house. She saw that her suitcase was beside the door, where Jeremiah must have put it while she slept, then continued to follow the music down the stairs.

She hadn't noticed the decor the night before, but Jeremiah's sprawling home was painted in warm Southern tones, with wooden furniture throughout the place. It was elegant, but so very country. She half expected to find a painting of a desert on one of the walls.

By the time she had made her way through the living room to the kitchen, she recognized the song and couldn't stop the smile that spread across her face. He was listening to *Sexy and I know it* by LMFAO.

She stepped into the kitchen doorway just as it reached the chorus, and was greeted with Jeremiah dancing at the stove, a spatula in his hand, singing along. His back was to her, so she stood and took in the scene without interrupting.

"I'm sexy and wiggle wiggle wiggle wiggle, yeah! Wiggle wiggle wiggle wiggle, yeah!" he sang, slightly offbeat.

He shook his jean-clad ass with every "wiggle," and she had no idea why it was sexy when it should have been absolutely ridiculous, but man, he had a nice ass.

Then he noticed her and turned down the music. "Was it too loud? Did I wake you?" he asked.

She shook her head. He didn't seem self-conscious at all about being caught wiggling with a spatula in his hand, which just made him even more adorable.

Sexy, not adorable, she reminded herself. And it was sexy, though how that was possible, she had no idea.

"Nice dancing," she commented.

He gave her a smile that turned her legs to jelly. "Yeah, I considered becoming a professional, but you know how it goes."

His eyes lit up as they raked over her from head to foot, lingering at the hem of the shirt that only just covered her. Her pulse sped up and she could feel heat flood her body. There seemed to be more than just shallow attraction in his expression, though. Something akin to contentment was mixed in with the desire in his eyes, and that made her hesitate. She wanted to say something sultry, to keep things flirty and sexy between them.

That was when she noticed what he was wearing over his clothes. It was a neon-green apron—covered in cats. Her train of thought veered wildly.

"You bought *yourself* one of those ugly aprons? I thought that thing was a joke you played on Aaron."

He looked down at the hideous item in question. "There was a sale going on. Buy one, get one half off."

She tried to stifle her laughter, but wasn't very successful. "You still paid money for it, though? Real dollars?"

He smiled and nodded. "I thought it was pretty bad at first, but it's grown on me. And the green looks way better than Aaron's pink one. And everyone loves cats."

His self-confidence amazed her. She'd never met

anyone so comfortable with themselves. How did he do that?

Jeremiah's voice broke into her thoughts. "Breakfast? I made waffles and sausage," he said, gesturing with his spatula.

Her stomach growled in response, and she sat at the table as he brought over a steaming plate that smelled absolutely delicious. She wasn't sure what made her mouth water more: the food, or the cook.

He caught her gaze as he set down the plate and gave her a look that liquefied her insides. The cook, definitely. Even in his silly apron.

A thought occurred to her as she doused her waffles in syrup. "Does Aaron know you have one of those aprons, too? He didn't talk like he did."

Jeremiah shook his head. "No, and you can't tell him. Otherwise I won't be able to tease him about it anymore, and what's the fun in that?"

She tried to come up with some reply, but her thoughts were distracted by the crispy, sweet creation she had just stuffed into her mouth. As soon as she swallowed, she shook her head. "What is it with you guys and amazing breakfast food? Is that a Texas thing?"

"No, it's a 'my mom' thing. She insisted I help with the cooking when I was a kid, and Aaron was over so often as we grew up that he learned, too. I can also make a mean chicken parm. And my snickerdoodles kick ass."

"Is there anything *not* awesome about you?" she asked. She said it jokingly, but in a way she was serious.

Why did this guy, the one who lived far away and she'd met at the worst possible time, have to be so absolutely perfect? Why couldn't he just be a sexy way to spend a week, no strings attached?

Because she hated to admit it, but strings were attaching all over the place, and it was going to hurt when all those strings broke.

"I can't roll my tongue, I always lose at Monopoly and you just saw my dancing. No more to say about that."

Dammit, none of those was bad enough. She took another bite, savoring the flavors and trying to push the worry out of her head. She would just need to enjoy the here and now, and prepare herself for the inevitable end of this whole thing.

As she looked around the kitchen, she noticed one strike against him. "Don't forget that you decorate with antlers."

Jeremiah looked at the antler chandelier hanging down from the ceiling. "Yeah, I guess it must seem pretty crazy to someone not from around here. It's just the way everything's always been and I never thought to change it when my parents moved out."

Jeremiah went back to the stove and got his own plate, then sat down beside her. He poured syrup on his waffle while he said, "So, did you want to go into town today and see some of the sights, or—"

"Or. Definitely or," she said, cutting him off.

He gave her a grin so full of promise that the temperature in the room went up by a few degrees. She resisted the urge to fan herself with her hand. This was what she'd wanted. No more of that gooey sweet

stuff. "Good," he said, "because there isn't really anything to see in town. I don't know what we'd do there."

"We can just stay here, then. I'm sure we can come
up with ways to pass the time," she responded with a
flirtatious raising of an eyebrow.

Jeremiah took one of her hands and brought it to his
mouth, biting lightly at her palm. The sensation shot
through her body, settling low in her stomach. "I have
a few ideas," he said.

She wanted to giggle like a schoolgirl. Yes, this was
going to be a good day.

When they were finished eating, she picked up the
plates and took them to the sink, aware that she was
giving him a good view of her backside as she did so.
By the way he cleared his throat and the flush on his
skin when she turned around, she was sure he'd taken
full advantage of the opportunity.

"Well, what should we do first? We have the entire
day free," she said as she walked back toward him,
aware of just how much of her legs was on display.

He held out his hand as if asking for help out of his
chair, but when she took it, he pulled her into his lap
instead of getting up himself. She could feel his body
hard against her in more ways than one.

"Well," he began, sliding the collar of her shirt off
one shoulder and nipping at her skin in a way that sent
bolts of pleasure through her. "I can think of a few different options."

His bites and kisses traveled across her exposed
shoulder and onto the base of her neck.

"Like what?" she asked in a hoarse whisper. She

tilted her head back to give him more access, and he immediately took advantage of it.

"We could play hours of Monopoly, or we could have sex."

His hands slid under the hem of the shirt and began moving along her body, leaving trails of heat wherever they touched.

"Hmmm, let me think about that," she said, her eyes closed as she enjoyed his attentions. "I actually hate Monopoly," she told him.

"Good. Me, too."

10

JEREMIAH SAT UP SLIGHTLY, looking up and down Renee's beautiful body, his fingers trailing along her side. She squirmed slightly at his touch and moved even closer to him. His heart slammed in his chest. Opening her eyes and stretching, she said, "I haven't taken a nap in years."

"How was it?"

She sat up and gave him a sleepy grin. "Wonderful. The US should really get on board with this *siesta* thing."

While he was watching her sleep, he'd been considering something, and now he came to a decision. He got up and started dressing. "I want to show you something, Renee."

She leaned on her elbow and looked at him, as if she was trying to figure out what was going on. He knew that getting closer frightened her, but he needed her to know about this side of him, even if she wasn't totally ready for the next step. For a moment, he thought she might refuse.

She nodded and rose, putting on clothes without a word.

His heart started pounding again, but this time for a different reason. Very few things made him nervous, but he was anxious about this. Still, he was going to go through with it, come what may. He wanted her to know about him, just like he wanted to know everything about her.

Once they were both dressed, he walked with her down the stairs and out the back door to a large old wooden shed that used to hold gardening supplies and other equipment. When they got there, he leaned against the door and looked at her.

She smiled at him, a little nervously, he thought. At least he wasn't the only one. He took a deep breath before opening the door and ushering her inside. Dust motes floated in the sunlight filtering through the windows around the room he'd turned into a studio, and here and there the light bounced off his statues, making colors dance on the ceiling.

Renee walked among them silently, studying each one with a deep solemnity, as if she was wandering through a cemetery. When she reached out and ran her hand along the edge of the one he called *Mother and Daughter*—two leaf-shaped pieces of copper, the larger curled around the smaller—he couldn't wait any longer. "What do you think?"

"You made these?" she asked.

He bit back his nerves, which he thought might break if she didn't give him her opinion. "I started a couple of years ago. I wanted to learn how to solder and cut different types of metal, so I practiced by making different designs and it just sort of turned into this," he said, sweeping his hand around the studio. "I know they're not great—"

"Are you kidding?" she said, interrupting him. "These are amazing. You're an artist."

All the tension eased out of his body. She liked them. "I wouldn't call myself an artist. It's a hobby."

He tried not to let her know how much it meant to him, but she seemed to know anyway. And her earlier reticence seemed to have disappeared. She touched another one, her fingers dancing across the overlapping aluminum squares. "You could sell these, you know. I'm sure you could."

How many times had he thought about trying to sell them? Hundreds, probably. He'd even gone so far as to research different places that might want to purchase them. But something always made him decide against it. "You think so?" he asked, his self-consciousness draining away.

She touched another one, her palm resting against the spidery slivers of wire that had taken so long to shape, and she moved around to see it from every angle. "I can't believe Jessica and Aaron haven't forced you to share these with the world. They're so beautiful."

When he didn't answer, Renee glanced up at him. He didn't need to say anything. "Why haven't you told your best friend about this?"

Jeremiah shrugged. "It's really personal. I don't think he'd get that."

"But you showed me," she said. It wasn't a question.

He nodded. There was so much he wanted to tell her. How much she meant to him, despite how short their time together had been. How this sort of thing didn't come along every day and they needed to see where it led.

But he didn't say any of that. Not yet. He didn't want to scare her away. Still, she must have seen some of it in his eyes, because she suddenly seemed nervous again and turned back to the statues, away from him. Her voice took on a light, friendly tone, in stark contrast to the quiet seriousness of a few moments before. "Well, I'd buy one for sure if I didn't live in a shoe-box-sized apartment," she said, standing next to one piece that was taller than her.

Jeremiah wanted to tell her to pick her favorite and it would be waiting here for her, but he stopped himself. The idea had too much future in it. She wasn't ready for future. Luckily, he was a master at keeping things light and carefree. Wasn't that what he'd done most of his life?

"Yeah, I guess I haven't really scaled them for New York City living. Maybe I should work on paperweight-sized ones. There's good money in the paperweight business, right?"

She seemed to appreciate the change in mood. "Oh yeah, paperweights are booming right now. People can use them to hold down their flash drives full of documents."

"Maybe I can make digital statues to hold down documents flying around in the cloud."

She chuckled and wandered around the last few

pieces with a lighter step. He leaned against the wall, not feeling very lighthearted at all. Why was she so scared to get close to him?

When she was finished studying each statue, they walked back to the house. He was glad he'd shown her, but couldn't help but feel like he was just setting himself up for heartbreak. Every time he tried to get closer to her, she pulled away. Did he need to be hit over the head to see that she wasn't interested in a long-term thing? Why couldn't he get that through his thick skull?

Still, he couldn't stop himself from hoping that over the next couple of days he could convince her to give this thing a shot. It was too good, too right, to be for just one week.

Once they were back in the house, Renee turned to him and gave him a devilish smile, and that was all he needed to put away those thoughts for another time. He would deal with all that later. For now, there was only one thing he wanted to think about.

He walked up close to her and placed one palm on the small of her back, pressing her against his body as his lips met hers. They had an entire day alone together, and he wasn't going to waste it.

"I HAVE BEEN waiting for this moment," Jeremiah said.

Renee gasped as his arm encircled her waist, pulling her tight against his body. She melted into his eyes as he leaned in, his soft kiss promising so much more.

Applause and cheers surrounded her, taking her attention away from the sinfully sexy man in front of her.

They were in the barn, standing under the decorated

arch. Renee looked down. The white fabric of her dress glittered in the light.

Renee sat up in bed, groaning. This was very bad. Her mind replayed the dream, and the feeling it evoked wasn't fear. It had been a happy dream, and *that* was what made her nervous.

She looked over at Jeremiah, able to just see him in the early dawn light. He was sleeping peacefully, and the sight of him made her blood rush with that insatiable desire she had felt since meeting him, despite the sexual escapades of the day before. But there was something else, too.

Her heart twisted in a tender way that made her want to jump out of the bed and get away as quickly as she could. She had a pretty good guess what that feeling was, and it was the exact feeling she didn't want to have. Not here.

Panic rose in her throat as she pictured herself in Jessica's shoes, living in a big country home in Texas, miles away from everyone and everything. Her dream job no more than a memory.

She couldn't let that happen to her. She wasn't going to be some Texas wife, whatever her feelings might be.

Suddenly antsy, she got out of bed and went to her suitcase lying open on the floor. Grabbing some clothes and her computer from her suitcase, she left the room and eased the bedroom door shut behind her.

Downstairs, she dressed and sat on the couch with her laptop. The best thing to do when her thoughts were jumbled like this was to work. It had gotten her through confusing and difficult times before; it would get her through this.

Renee opened the page she had begun to design and started her tweaks. She wished she had gotten Jessica's article and the photo onto her computer before leaving so she could have them in place while working on the page, but she had noted the length of the article and had the picture imprinted in her mind, so she could create the mock-up without them.

If she wanted this to look good, it would take time. Luckily, time was what she had, and she desperately wanted to fill it with something other than thoughts about Jeremiah and a future with him that couldn't possibly work.

She settled in, her eyes glued to the screen, and got down to business.

JEREMIAH BEGAN TO WAKE, but he felt so content and comfortable that he was in no hurry to get out of bed. With his eyes closed, he reached out to Renee to pull her closer. His hand only met empty space where he expected warm skin, though, and he opened his eyes. She wasn't in bed, and based on the cool spot beside him, she had been gone for a while.

He rose and threw on some clothes, wondering where she had gone and what she could be doing. The thought of her cooking breakfast made him chuckle. If she was, he'd happily eat her toast, burned or not.

When he got downstairs, he found her in the living room, not the kitchen, and felt slightly relieved. If she was as bad at cooking as she claimed, it was better that way. He started running through his list of possible meal options, trying to decide which one she'd like the most. He loved the way she looked when she bit into something delicious.

As he walked up to her from behind the couch, he could see her laptop on her knees, a magazine page blossoming on the screen. She was absorbed in what she was doing and hadn't seen him yet, so he stood for a minute and watched her work, adding lines and tiny details to the page that elevated it from a regular magazine page to an eye-catching design akin to a piece of art. It was still in an infancy stage, but he could see the final product shining through, and he was impressed.

His eyes shifted from studying the screen to the woman in front of it. Her hair was falling forward into her face, but she didn't seem to notice. Her entire being seemed focused on what she was doing, absorbed in her work. He wondered if he'd be able to create a statue that would capture the drive and focus she exuded from every line of her form.

Finally, he walked up to her and knelt behind the couch, only inches from her. "You really have a talent," he said.

She jumped, startled, and looked over at him. He gave her a smile, but it took her a couple of beats before she returned it, and his stomach turned unpleasantly. Something had changed since the night before. He didn't know exactly why, but a feeling of foreboding washed over him.

"Are you hungry?" he asked, hoping to dispel the unpleasant thought.

She nodded and turned back to her screen, not looking at him. "Yeah, but I need to get a little more work done."

"I'll whip up some omelets," he said, rising from the back of the couch.

"You don't *have* to, but I can't say no to that offer."

Her words were pleasant, but she still wasn't looking at him and her voice had the quality of someone reading from a script. He went into the kitchen and began working on breakfast while his mind tried to work through what might have changed since last night.

As he chopped, whisked and flipped, he managed to come up with a few theories, but nothing seemed to make sense, except that for some reason she'd decided to put more distance between them. It made his heart sink to think that she might be done with him, satisfied with her fling and ready to walk away.

His suspicions only grew when she came into the kitchen for breakfast. After politely thanking him for the meal, she said, "I should move back to Jessica and Aaron's today. I need to help with the last few wedding items, and the rest of the guests will be starting to arrive."

He chewed a bite, then swallowed. "What's going on, Renee?" he asked.

He needed to know. She finally managed to look him in the eyes. "I just think this shouldn't go any further. We've had our fun, but now I need to get back to reality. Finish my project for work and help Jessica."

He considered arguing with her, but let it go for the moment. They ate in silence, and once she was done she pushed back from the table. "I'll wash the dishes. Then will you take me back to Jessica's?"

"Is that really what you want?"

She gave him a forced smile. "Well, I'm not the biggest fan of washing dishes, but it seems only fair," she said.

He knew that move too well. He'd done it plenty of times, and he wasn't about to let her off the hook.

"That's not what I meant, and you know it."

She turned her back to him, as if she didn't want him to see her face, and began running water over the dirty dishes. "I think it's best for both of us if I get back to helping Jessica prepare for the wedding. It's why I'm here, after all."

Jeremiah opened his mouth to say something, but after a moment he closed it again. What was there to say? What she said was true. If she didn't want anything more than a quick fling, it would be better for them to stop before he got in so deep he couldn't get out again.

Not that he was by any means certain that hadn't already happened.

He watched as she finished washing the dishes and left the kitchen to gather her things, avoiding his gaze the entire time. When she left the house with her suitcase in hand, he followed.

RENEE HATED EVERY second of the drive back to Jessica and Aaron's, which was all the more reason to leave Jeremiah's. She couldn't risk losing the willpower needed to break things off with him, and the more time she spent around him, the worse it would be. Better to get it over with now.

She wasn't sure if the drive felt like an eternity or far too short, but once they pulled up to the house, everything in her shouted to stay in the car, go back with Jeremiah and forget about all that other stuff.

She had to get out of that truck as fast as she could. Renee took off her seat belt and was about to open the door, but Jeremiah turned to her, the determination in his eyes pinning her in place. Renee willed him to just let her leave. No discussion, no explanation.

He put his hand on hers. "I want more than just this week, Renee," he said.

Renee's insides twisted painfully. She wanted to run away, but couldn't.

"One week isn't enough for me. I think this has a shot."

He looked at her with such sincerity that her heart melted a little, but she forced it to freeze over. There was too much at stake. Her career, the city she loved, her life. She couldn't let herself fall in love with this guy and lose all those things that were so important to her.

He seemed to be waiting for an answer. When she didn't say anything, he asked, "Don't you think we have something here?"

She pulled her hand out from under his and turned to the door so he wouldn't see the hurt in her eyes, the lie on her lips. "No, I don't."

Before he could say anything else, she had the door open and was out in the brisk morning air. She made her way to the house as quickly as she could, praying he wouldn't come after her before she could make it to the door. She wasn't sure what she would say if he did.

Her resolve could only last so long against those coffee-colored eyes.

When she made it inside the house without his intervention, Renee told herself what she felt was relief, though she wasn't quite sure she believed it. She took a deep breath to calm her roiling emotions, and hoped her face belied the truth festering underneath when Jessica appeared.

Clearly it didn't, as her sister's expression changed immediately from welcoming to worry. "What happened, Renee? Are you okay?"

Renee didn't want to deceive her sister again. There had just been too many lies lately. But she couldn't bring herself to explain the situation with Jeremiah, either. "I fell and hurt myself," she said.

It wasn't really a lie at all. Jessica looked at her with concern. "Are you okay?"

Renee said, "I will be," hoping it was the truth.

Without another word, Jessica ushered Renee into the kitchen and got her a cup of tea. Renee sipped the hot liquid, trying to settle her feelings. Aaron walked in from outside, carrying her suitcase. "Jeremiah just left. He asked me to bring in your bag," he said to Renee.

"He left without coming in? That's weird," Jessica said.

Aaron shrugged. "I know. I expected him to offer to stick around and help with everything today, but he said he was busy."

Renee didn't say anything, just took another swallow of her drink and tried to convince herself that it was good he left. It was over now.

She took one more swallow and grabbed her bag. "I'm going to get some work done before we get started on wedding stuff, if that's okay," she told them.

Jessica said, "That's fine. The tent guys should be here in an hour or so. Once it's up, we can get everything ready for the reception. You'll have some time to work this afternoon, too, when Aaron and I head over to the airport. Cindy and Mom and Stew are flying in today."

Renee remembered Jessica's freak-out over the phone about Stew coming to the wedding. It was just a few days ago, but felt so much longer. At any rate, Jessica seemed to have accepted his presence at the wedding.

Renee gathered her suitcase, the camera and—with only a little reluctance on Jessica's part—the article she planned to use in her spread design, then went up to her room and settled herself at the desk in the corner of the room, determined to get down to work.

She got everything she needed loaded onto her computer, then stared at the screen. She usually felt a level of excitement when she was putting the pieces together and perfecting her design, but she didn't feel that at all. She felt...

Sad. That was the only word she could come up with to describe it.

Her work had always helped her get over any negative emotions, and she was sure it could now. She just needed to focus. She put her hands to the keyboard, telling herself to just get started already.

She began clicking through various icons, opening Jessica's article and the picture she had taken. Her hands fell from the keyboard as she stared at the picture. It wasn't the barn or the brilliant sky or any of a hundred other aspects of the photograph that caught her attention. It was Jeremiah.

The picture only showed him from the back as he helped Aaron slide open the large door, but it was enough to render her speechless. His mop of dark hair was messy in a shaggy-chic kind of look, and his shirt was slightly wrinkled, as if he'd been working all day doing manly things, but she knew the truth of those little details.

They were like that because Renee had been riding him up in the loft not long before the photo was taken.

God, he looked good.

She closed the laptop with a snap and stood. She just needed some air and a couple of minutes to get her head in order, and then she'd be fine.

Before she could examine the idea too closely, she was on her way out the door she had just entered minutes before.

She saw Jessica and Aaron sitting in the living room as she passed from the stairs to the front door, but she didn't say anything and they didn't try to follow her, which was a relief. She just needed to be alone.

Well, not alone. You need to be with Jeremiah.

She hushed the voice in her head, dismissing the thought. She did *not* need him. She didn't need anyone. As long as she got this dream job, she would have everything she needed to be happy.

Yeah, right.

She had really started to hate that voice.

Renee walked as quickly as she could, trying to out-run it. It was only when she found the sun blocked by leaves that she realized she had walked into the shade of the trees behind the barn. She kept walking, breathing in the cool, wet air, until she heard the burble of a stream. It had to be the river she and Jeremiah had pretended to visit.

After a few more steps, she could see it. Shafts of light broke through the leafy ceiling and landed on the water, creating shining reflections on the surface. The spots where the water broke over rocks made it sound happy, as if the water was giggling.

A small smile touched Renee's lips. She really *did* like the tiny waterfalls. At least that was one less lie she had on her conscience.

The sound of the water was soothing, and she walked along beside the stream until her fingers felt stiff from the cold morning air. When she finally broke through the trees once more, she saw a group of men setting up the tent where the wedding reception would be held. It was huge and pure white, with windows dotting the sides.

Jeremiah's voice rose up in her mind. *The circus fire was intense. Get it?*

She chuckled, but wasn't sure the emotion she was feeling could be called amusement. Before more thoughts of him could overwhelm her good sense, Renee blanked her mind and went to find Jessica. If anyone could keep her so busy that she didn't have time to think of those coffee-colored eyes, that delicious body and adorable smile, it was Jessica.

Her sister was standing near the tent, watching as it grew to full height. Renee guessed Jessica was going over every inch of it with her eyes, looking for some tiny tear that might get caught by a gust of wind and somehow cause the entire thing to fall apart.

She pasted on a smile as she approached her sister. No sense in making her worry. "It's a beautiful tent, Jessica. It looks like everything is going according to plan."

Jessica nodded, but didn't seem fully convinced, though Renee wasn't sure if her sister was concerned about the wedding or about Renee.

Either way, Jessica said nothing and Renee didn't press her to find out.

In short order, the tent was in place and the horde of workers had packed up and gone, leaving the large, empty structure behind. Renee turned to Jessica. "What's first? Tables? Where are they?"

Jessica eyed her, as if she was suspicious. "Yes, but we can wait for Aaron, and he can call Jeremiah to see if he can help—"

"No!" Renee interrupted before realizing how odd it must seem. "I mean, we can lift a few tables without the guys. Strong, independent women and all that."

The "few tables" ended up being ten huge round ones that had to weigh a hundred pounds each, along with a dozen rectangular ones that weren't much lighter. Within fifteen minutes, both women were out of breath and sweating, despite the chilly morning air. Jessica and Renee dragged and rolled the tables until each one was in place.

Renee wished there were even more of them. Nothing like a little heavy lifting to stop the mind from wandering into forbidden territory.

The moment they were done, Jessica sat down on the ground, her face red, and she took a big breath. "Well that was fun."

Renee dropped to the ground beside her. "It wasn't that bad."

Jessica didn't answer, and they rested for a minute, looking around the tent. The circular tables were spread out over most of the space, waiting to become seating for the guests. Rectangular tables were relegated to the perimeter, where they would hold the cake, food and gifts. There was still so much to do before it would be ready, but Renee could picture how it would look, and it was beautiful.

Her heart ached a little and she felt a burning behind her eyes that couldn't possibly be tears. She stood again and turned away from her sister. "What's next? Chairs?"

From behind her, Jessica said, "You're kidding, right? Don't you want to take a little break? We have time."

Renee absolutely did not want a break. Breaks were when thoughts and feelings could intrude. Better to keep working. "Where are the chairs?" she asked in response.

Jessica heaved herself up with a groan and led Renee to the barn. Her eyes immediately flew to the loft as images swam to the surface of her mind, but she shoved them back into the past where they belonged and brought her eyes back to ground level. The chairs were standing bunched in a corner, as out of the way as fifty or so large and starkly white chairs could get. They must have been delivered the day before, Renee realized. While she was at Jeremiah's.

Before more unwelcome images could come calling, she grabbed a chair and started moving. They were heavy, not cheap fold-away chairs by any stretch of the imagination. Renee could feel her muscles burning, but she ignored them.

After they had moved nearly half the chairs, Aaron showed up. "I didn't realize you two were going to start all the heavy lifting without me or I would've been quicker with the horses," he said.

Jessica went over to him, settling into his arms like they had been made for her. She said something Renee couldn't quite catch, but she assumed it was about her pushing them to get things done. And what was wrong with that?

With Aaron helping, the job sped up, and soon all the chairs were in the tent, encircling the tables. Renee was about to ask what the next job was, but before she could, Jessica was shaking her head. "Nope, I'm calling a lunch break. We've done enough for right now and I'm starving."

Renee didn't feel hungry at all, but what could she say? She shut her mouth and followed her sister back to the house.

11

JEREMIAH SAT ON his couch, the silence of the empty house heavy in his ears. Renee was gone. And she had made it perfectly clear that she was done with him and their whatever-it-was. He had tried to make her believe that they had a future, but it didn't work, and her "No" as she left the truck still sat on his chest like a heavy weight crushing everything beneath it.

Now that he was home, he knew there was plenty he could do to distract himself, to stop his mind from going back to its favorite topic, Renee, but instead he sat on the couch.

Maybe if he could talk to her, really explain how he felt and why she should give them a chance, she would see the truth in it. They were great together. In the bedroom and out. He couldn't just let that all go so easily, could he?

But he'd need some kind of gesture, something more than just words. An idea formed in his mind. It would take time, but if he started immediately, it should be ready by tomorrow evening, the rehearsal dinner.

He stood and rushed to his studio, a determined smile on his lips.

RENEE HEARD THE sound of tires on gravel through her window and shut her laptop. She had managed to paste in the article Jessica had written and adjust the layout design to match the length. She had also added the picture of the men opening the front door of the barn.

Those things would normally take less than a half hour, but it was over two hours since she had sat down to work. She hadn't been able to find her focus.

She was also missing the sense of accomplishment that usually came when she completed a task for a layout.

Renee ran her fingers through her hair. Work had always been there for her, and now, when she most needed it, she felt dissatisfied.

She pushed away from the desk and headed downstairs. The babble of overlapping voices coming from outside grew louder as Jessica, Aaron and the newcomers approached the house.

As Renee moved to the front door, it burst open, and Renee's mother entered, all smiles. She was followed by her boyfriend, Stew; Jessica's best friend, Cindy; and Cindy's husband. The bustle was a welcome relief. If she was busy talking and catching up, maybe she could forget about the way Jeremiah's eyes sparkled when he was happy, or the way they dug into her soul when he was earnest.

After chatting into the evening, however, Jeremiah was no closer to disappearing from her brain. The only thing her attempt at distraction did was give her a headache. Pretending to be happy and pleasant was more work than she'd thought.

Finally, she couldn't take it any longer. "I think I'm going to head up to bed," she said, hoping she would get out of the room without much argument.

"Are you okay, Renee? You look pale," her mother said, concerned.

Renee shrugged. "I just have a bit of a headache."

Boy, was that the understatement of the year.

Everyone sent her to bed with well wishes, making Renee feel even crappier. All these loving, sweet people were here for Jessica's wedding, and she couldn't even pull it together for them? Over a guy she had no future with?

She dropped into bed, her stomach roiling with unpleasant emotions.

ANOTHER SLEEPLESS NIGHT and it was the day of the rehearsal dinner. Renee spent the day staying as busy as possible, determined to stick out the entire day and not let herself pine over something so tiny that didn't feel tiny at all. Everyone helped to decorate the tables for the reception and get everything ready for the rehearsal dinner celebration that evening. With everyone working together, though, it was finished in a few hours, and Renee had run out of things to do.

She steeled herself to make small talk and be a perfectly pleasant helper to Jessica, even though her heart wasn't in it. Luckily, Jessica came up and put a hand on her shoulder the moment the last table setting was in place. "Renee, you still look a little ill. I think you should take a break before the rehearsal dinner."

Renee was about to protest, but Jessica shook her head before she could say a word. "Go take a nap or something. Please."

The concern on Jessica's face tugged at Renee's heartstrings, and she threw her arms around Jessica and squeezed her tight. "Thanks, sister. I love you."

She hoped Jessica wouldn't ask Renee to explain any of her odd behaviors, and felt relieved when Jessica hugged her back and only said, "Love you, too. Now go get some rest."

Renee didn't need to be asked twice; she was exhausted.

The moment she dropped onto the bed, however, she sat back up. There was just too much Jeremiah in this bed for her to be comfortable. Instead, she grabbed her laptop and decided to bury herself in her favorite distraction—work.

The rehearsal dinner would be starting in a couple of hours, and Renee was sure she wouldn't have an opportunity to get much done until after the wedding the next day, so this was the best time to get some work in.

When Renee sat down at the desk with her computer, though, she couldn't find the motivation to get started. Why was she even putting herself through this? She had plenty of great pages that showed off her skills. She didn't need to make a new one.

And even if she still wanted to submit the new page,

did she really need to put in hours of work to make it just a tiny bit better? She opened what she had done so far. It wasn't perfect, but it was very good already. Certainly good enough.

Renee shook her head. When had she ever thought something was "good enough"? She wasn't sure what had happened to her, but she knew exactly who it was that had started it. Jeremiah.

She hadn't seen him since she'd climbed out of his truck two days ago, but that didn't mean his presence hadn't been felt for those two days. In fact, now that she let herself admit it, all that time she'd spent with her mind blank, when she was hauling heavy tables into place and chatting with her mother, Jeremiah had been front and center, whatever she tried to do.

This fun fling, this impractical relationship, was making it impossible for her to do her job. Renee's frustration came out as she slammed down the lid of her laptop and paced around the room.

Jeremiah would be at the rehearsal dinner, and this was the time to end things once and for all. She needed to burn that bridge so it would stop beckoning to her, inviting her to cross into Texas housewife territory.

If she did, there would be no going back. Her career, her life in New York, were all too important to risk. If she needed to lose a bit of her heart in the process, well, then that was a sacrifice she was willing to make.

JEREMIAH COULD FEEL his heart in his throat as he climbed out of his truck. He touched the bulge of his chest pocket, gathering strength from it. He would give

Renee the gift as a peace offering, and then perhaps she would reconsider their relationship. Even if it was just temporary.

Temporary was better than nothing, and maybe it would be able to turn into something more. He could imagine her reaction to his present, and the thought of it made his heart beat faster. He was sure she would love it, and if he gave it to her in private, maybe they could have their own little party before rejoining the rehearsal dinner.

He walked along the side of Jessica and Aaron's house, following the light and noise, excitement making his pace nearly a jog. Now that he was here, he couldn't get to Renee soon enough. Behind the house, two dozen or so people were gathered, talking in small clumps. Large heaters were spaced throughout the crowd to keep away the chill that had been in the air the entire day, and everyone seemed happy and comfortable. The smell of barbecue and music filled the air.

The rehearsal dinner looked just as Jessica had described it: long tables laden with classic Texas barbecue and sides, friends and family mingling. He saw Jessica and Aaron surrounded by people they cared about, smiling and laughing, and felt lighter for a moment. At least this whole thing with Renee hadn't ruined anything for them.

And if he was lucky and things worked out, he was sure they would be happy about him and Renee being together.

Now he just needed to convince Renee.

Jeremiah's eyes found her almost immediately, standing beside an older version of herself and a man who looked like an elderly professor. It had to be her mom and the boyfriend, whom he had heard about from Jessica.

Before he could walk up to her and ask her for a private word, Renee saw him and hurried over. His heart jumped at the sight. *Maybe she finally sees that we have something bigger than a fling,* he thought.

Once she got closer, though, her eyes and expression turned his hope to worry. She didn't look happy to see him—she looked exhausted. And determined.

She left the circle of light and music and gaiety, striding ever closer, and suddenly he didn't want her to get any nearer. He could see from her face that whatever she planned to say or do, it wouldn't be good. The excitement that had been building in him died.

Renee stopped several feet away from him, out of arm's reach. Before he could say anything, she said, "I wanted to let you know before you entered the party that I still don't want anything more to happen between us, just in case you were considering trying to discuss it with me. I've sowed my wild oats, and now it's over. We're done. Please leave it at that."

She didn't look him in the eyes once, and she left without his saying a word.

RENEE WALKED AWAY, wondering what she would do if Jeremiah stopped her, if he saw the tears in her eyes. She hadn't wanted to be harsh, but it was the only way to cut things off for good. Why did she have to say that thing about wild oats, like he was nothing to her?

You had to. He'd keep pushing otherwise.

Still, she couldn't stop thinking about how much that must have hurt him, and she knew that this had to be the last time she let herself get close to him. She'd only allowed herself one glance at him before turning away, but the pain on his face in that second had hit her like a punch to the gut, and she couldn't let herself fall into his arms again, only to hurt him another time. It was clear that he wanted far more than she could give, which was all the more reason to stay away from him altogether.

If luck was on her side, she thought, he would keep his distance until the wedding was over, and then she could go home and retreat into her work, into her little New York life, and that would be that. He could find a sweet girl who would be happy to live on a ranch in Texas, living the content country life, and she would…

Well, she would have her dream job. That would need to be enough.

She rejoined her mother and Stew. "What was that about, Renee?" the older woman asked once Renee was with them once again.

Renee tried to give a convincing smile. "I just needed to talk to Jeremiah real quick about something. For the wedding."

She left it at that, hoping her mother would drop the subject, and her stomach felt knotted with tension. Once this weekend was over, Renee was done with lying, that was for sure.

For a moment it seemed like her mother would ask another question, but then she turned back to discussing the cruise she and Stew would be taking in a few weeks.

Renee breathed out a secret sigh of relief and tried to focus her attention on the two people in front of her, not the one she had left on the edge of the party.

JEREMIAH LEFT THE circle of light and walked around near the horse paddock, avoiding the merriment of the rehearsal dinner. Ever since her very clear dismissal, Renee refused to even look at him, and it was driving him nuts. He could feel the object he'd brought for her weighing down his breast pocket, and now he felt stupid working so hard to have it ready in time. He took it out and looked at it.

He had made her a miniature statue of copper and silver pieces intertwined in a tiny dance. He knew she would like it, but how could he give it to her now? She wasn't going to let him get close enough to talk to her, let alone willingly follow him to somewhere private so he could at least hand it to her.

She had made it incredibly clear that she wanted nothing more to do with him, and now he was stuck at this party, watching her ignore him and feeling the weight of his gift like an albatross around his neck.

The nearest horse snorted at him, and he reached out and patted her nose. It was chilly away from the heaters that protected the party from the cold, but he didn't care. At least if he stayed away from the whole thing, he wouldn't have to constantly be hit over the head by the fact that she was completely done with him.

And then a distraction came along in the form of a brunette wearing glasses. "Jeremiah!" she called out, rushing over to him and giving him a big hug.

He returned the embrace, trying to push Renee from his mind and give her a genuine smile. It was an impossible task. "Hi, Kiki. I didn't think you were going to be able to make it."

"I wasn't sure I would, but I managed to wrap everything up in time. I flew in last week, but you know how my mom is. This is the first time I've had a chance to see anybody since I got back."

"It'll be good to have you around for a bit," he said.

She stared at his face intently for a moment. "How are you?" she asked, concern edging her voice.

How could she already tell something was wrong?

Before he could respond, Kiki's infamous mother appeared as if from nowhere. "I was wondering where you disappeared off to, Kerstin. You really should go visit with Aaron and the bride for a bit. He is your cousin, after all, and it's rude not to chat with her some," the older woman said while pushing Kiki's hair out of her eyes.

Jeremiah watched Kiki's controlled expression and wondered how hard it was for her to keep from rolling her eyes. If he hadn't been feeling so crappy, he would have found this to be pretty amusing.

"I already talked to them, Mom, and set up a lunch date with Jessica for after their honeymoon. I thought it would be better to let them talk to their out-of-town guests right now," Kiki said.

"Oh pshaw," her mother returned. "You're their *family*. I'm sure they would love it if you sat down with them for a bit."

Jeremiah wondered if Kiki would point out that all

those other guests were also family, but instead she gestured at Jeremiah. "I can't right now, Mom. Jeremiah just asked me to dance and I said I would. It would be rude to go back on my word."

Her mother seemed disappointed, but said nothing. The last thing Jeremiah wanted to do was dance, but he couldn't leave Kiki in the lurch. They had been friends since grade school, and he was sure she would do the same for him. He took her hand and moved closer to the music, away from her mother's stifling presence.

Once they were dancing, she said, "Thanks. I owe you one."

"Your mom hasn't changed one bit, has she?"

Kiki shook her head, her lips pursed with what had to be unpleasant reflections. He thought it best to change the subject. "How was Beijing?"

Her expression smoothed into a small smile. "It was great. But we can talk about that later. Let's talk about you first. For instance, we can talk about what has you so down in the dumps."

He had thought he'd been pulling it off pretty well. He wasn't ready to talk about the whole Renee thing quite yet, however. Not with her sitting twenty feet away. Maybe once she was back in New York. Though Beijing was probably not far enough away to get her out of his mind, let alone New York.

Kiki seemed to sense his reluctance because she said, "Okay, different question—are you still playing the field? Sowing wild oats?"

Jeremiah had to smile. The humor of the situation

wasn't lost on him. "No, I'm ready to settle down, I think."

"With a strawberry blonde bridesmaid?" Kiki asked, though by her tone it was clear she already knew the answer.

Jeremiah stopped dancing. "How did you know?"

Kiki smiled and shook her head. "You're easy to read, Jeremiah."

He shouldn't be surprised. She'd always been observant. "Yeah, well, she was just having fun and now she's over it. I knew she wasn't looking for anything serious from the beginning, but I let myself get in a little too deep. I'm getting what I deserve, I guess."

Kiki looked at him like he had just said the dumbest thing she'd ever heard. "You're kidding, right?"

He tried to figure out what she was thinking, but gave up. "What, Kiki?"

"You think that the woman who keeps looking at me like I stole her Christmas present was just in it for a little fun? Are you serious?"

Jeremiah seemed to be having trouble processing her words. "Stole her Christmas present?" he repeated.

"And knocked down the tree. And then set the house on fire. Still not clear enough? She definitely doesn't like that I'm dancing with you, Jeremiah."

Hope bloomed in his chest. "You think she's not done with me?"

Kiki slapped her own forehead. "I thought you were a pretty smart guy. Stop proving me wrong. Either she wants more than a fling and has some serious feelings for you, or she's crazy and a little scary."

RENEE WISHED SHE could magically transport herself away from this rehearsal dinner, but she was stuck forcing pleasant conversation with her mom and Stew when she felt anything but pleasant. She felt on edge and sleep deprived, and now she had to watch Jeremiah dance with a pretty brunette.

The worst thing about that was the knowledge that she had no right to dislike the way that woman smiled at Jeremiah. After all, Renee had told him they were finished, so what could she do but watch him move on to someone else?

Even though they were outside, she felt claustrophobic. She needed space to breathe. She turned her attention back to her mom, who was looking at her expectantly. She'd clearly missed something in the conversation and had no idea what kind of a reply was expected of her.

"I'm sorry, Mom, but I just thought of something I need to go take care of real quick. I'll be right back."

It wasn't great, but her mom nodded and Renee excused herself from the table. She needed a few minutes alone, and then she'd be able to handle the rest of the evening.

Renee made her way into and through the house, wanting nothing more than to flop on the bed, grab one of the pillows and breathe in the smell of it. Her body felt heavy, and she gave a sigh of relief once she finally made it to the top of the stairs.

She opened the door to her room and had taken a couple of steps before she registered that someone else was already there. Jeremiah was sitting on the edge of the bed, watching her with those deep brown eyes that threatened to swallow her whole. His presence was almost overwhelming, and she didn't know if she felt more anxious or relieved by his having him there.

She should ask him to leave. It was her room after all, at least for right now. Or she could just walk right back out and go somewhere else. Either option would be better than being in a room alone with him. She knew that. Instead, she closed the door behind her and walked farther into the room.

When he pulled her down to sit beside him on the bed, she did, and when he kissed her, all she could do was kiss him back. Her entire body was screaming out for her to be in his arms, and any little voice telling her it was a bad idea was shouted down. It felt so good to kiss him. She felt drunk from the sensation.

After a few seconds, he pulled away and rested his forehead against hers. "I've wanted to do that all evening. It's been torture being so near you and not kissing you," he said.

"You looked like you were having fun dancing," Renee said, trying to sound casual.

Jeremiah smirked and she knew he saw right through her. She flushed with embarrassment.

"That was Kiki, Aaron's cousin. She asked me to dance with her so she could get away from her mother."

Relief flooded her. "Not an ex-girlfriend," she said.

"Well, yeah, that, too."

The relief turned icy in her veins, but then Jeremiah laughed. "We dated for about a week when we were thirteen."

He pushed the hair away from her face, sending tendrils of desire through her. Her heart pounded in her chest. "So, not exactly the romance of the century?"

He smirked at her again. She wasn't sure if she wanted to punch his arm or kiss the look right off his face. Perhaps both in quick succession. "No," he answered, shifting even closer to her, making it difficult for her to breathe. "Aaron was so pissed when I broke up with her and made her cry. That's when I learned not to fool around with his family."

She stared at him, waiting for him to hear what he'd just said. His smile didn't change. "What about me?" she finally asked.

He touched her fingers lightly with his own, then moved them slowly up her arm. "Doesn't count."

She didn't know exactly what he meant, but she didn't care. All her attention was focused on his soft caress. All the resolutions she had made such a short time ago melted under those warm hands.

JEREMIAH KNEW THIS was his one opportunity to convince her to give them a chance. He had to tell her the whole truth before she remembered that she wanted nothing to do with him. He took a deep breath. "I've always tried to go for the things I want. It's been kind of a life philosophy—"

"That explains why you ever thought it was a good idea to ask out that supermodel," Renee mumbled, almost as if she was talking to herself.

He stopped talking, thrown off by her comment. How did she know about that?

"Aaron told us the whole story," she explained. "I'm pretty sure he tells it to everyone. It's pretty funny. How long was it until you were able to walk normally again?"

"Over a month," he grumbled, making her laugh.

"Anyway," he began again, trying to get back on track. He needed to just say it, so he plunged in headlong. "I'm in love with you, Renee."

She stilled and stared at him. Jeremiah, always so confident, had never felt less sure of himself. He might have just ruined any chance of easing her into a relationship, but after what Kiki had told him, and how he'd felt when he thought there was a possibility she had feelings for him, he knew he needed to tell her the truth. He'd been in love with her since he first saw her, and now she finally knew.

Silence stretched between them.

At last, Renee opened her mouth. Jeremiah held his breath, waiting for her response. "It's…a joke, right?"

He'd never felt more serious in his life, and as he realized that this conversation was not going to end the way he hoped, all he wanted was for it to be over. For a second, he considered lying and pretending he'd been kidding, but he couldn't do it, even if it would save him embarrassment. Renee deserved only honesty. "No joke," he said, trying to smile and shrug.

Renee covered her face with her hands and shook her head. "I can't," she said, her voice muffled by her hands.

Jeremiah stood.

He took out the small object that had been weighing down his chest pocket and set it on the bed where he had just been sitting. "For your shoe box apartment," he said.

Then he turned and walked out of the room, shutting the door behind him.

12

THE REHEARSAL DINNER was winding down, and most people had gone home. Jeremiah stood outside the circle of lights, away from the merriment. Renee hadn't come back down to the party after their disastrous talk, and he wasn't sure if that was a relief or not.

Kiki walked up to him and gave him a hug. "It's good to see you, Jeremiah."

"Good to see you, too, Kiki. I'm glad you're back."

"Your talk with the bridesmaid didn't work out, I take it?"

There was no point to asking how she knew. He was sure it was pretty obvious that something was wrong with him; he just couldn't force himself to pretend to be his normal happy-go-lucky self when he felt anything but. She shook her head in sympathy. "If there's any way I can help, let me know. I'll be in town for a while. You know where to find me." She gave him one last hug and left, her mother chattering beside her.

Aaron came up to Jeremiah after Kiki had disappeared and slapped his shoulder. "You ready to go?" he asked.

Jeremiah had never been more ready for anything in his life. "Let's go," he said.

They went to Jeremiah's car, where Jessica was waiting. Aaron's overnight bag was sitting on the ground by her feet.

Aaron pulled her into an embrace. "I'll see you tomorrow, wifey."

Jeremiah got into his truck, allowing the couple their private goodbye. After a couple of minutes, Aaron climbed into the passenger seat and Jeremiah turned the key. Aaron rolled down the window and planted one last kiss on his bride-to-be, and then they were on their way.

Jeremiah tried to behave normally, for his friend's sake. "What made you two decide to do the whole 'night apart' thing? I didn't think you would be able to tear yourselves away from each other for that long."

"You only get married once. Or, at least, I do. So we're doing it right."

Jeremiah nodded and tried to think of something to say. Before he could think of anything, Aaron said, "So, you're still not going to talk to me about what's going on with you until after tomorrow?"

"Yep."

Then he would tell Aaron the truth about the whole thing. But until Renee was back in New York and Jessica was a happily married woman, he was keeping mum.

"Well, let me just say that whatever's happening, you need to fix it so you can get back to being your normal self. I've never seen you this tense and unhappy. It's not like you."

Why can't I be unhappy sometimes? Do I always have to be the jokester? Jeremiah kept the thoughts to himself. He couldn't snap at Aaron like that the night before his wedding. And he knew that he wasn't even annoyed at Aaron; he was annoyed with himself and the universe that would let him fall so hard for someone who refused to love him back.

Aaron said, "I don't expect you to be funny all the time or anything, I just want you to not be perpetually bummed out."

Jeremiah wasn't surprised that Aaron knew what he was thinking. They had been best friends for thirty years, after all. But he still didn't want to talk. "Why don't you tell me about the honeymoon?"

There was a beat of silence, and Jeremiah waited for Aaron to point out that he already knew about the honeymoon, but Aaron didn't. Instead, he filled the rest of the drive with the honeymoon itinerary. As they pulled into Jeremiah's driveway, he said, "I can't believe the flight is the day after tomorrow."

Jeremiah tried to muster up as much enthusiasm for Aaron as he could. "You're getting married tomorrow. I hope you're ready."

By the goofy grin on his friend's face, Jeremiah was sure his friend was more than ready.

RENEE OPENED HER eyes and squinted at the rectangle of light coming in her bedroom door, not moving from her prone position on the bed. Jessica was standing there, looking concerned. "I wondered where you had disappeared to."

Renee sat up with a sigh. She hadn't been asleep, but at least in the quiet darkness of her room, she'd been able to pretend she was back in New York, away from everything that was so confusing.

She ran her hand through her hair, trying to pull herself together, not an easy feat under her sister's unwavering gaze. "Sorry I left the party early. I was tired."

"Still not ready to talk about it with me, huh?" Jessica asked as she stepped into the room, sitting on the bed where Jeremiah had sat not very long before.

Renee thought about it. For a moment, she considered spilling everything to her sister, telling her everything that had happened. But she couldn't do that the night before the wedding. What if Jessica was mad at her? Renee couldn't be the one to ruin the wedding.

Or worse, what if Jessica pushed her to talk to Jeremiah again? Renee didn't think she was strong enough to say no again. Not with those wonderful eyes staring at her, through her, as if they knew everything she wanted—

"Renee?" Jessica's voice cut into her thoughts.

She turned her attention back to her sister. "We can talk after the wedding."

Once she was back in New York and far away from Jeremiah's dangerously inviting arms.

Jessica still didn't look convinced. Renee smiled at her sister's stubborn nature. "I promise. We'll have a sisterly heart-to-heart when all this is done. Until then, all I want to do is celebrate your wedding with you. Okay?"

Jessica nodded and gave her a small smile back. "Fine. I won't ask you again until after the wedding. Now get some sleep. Tomorrow's the big day, you know."

With that, Jessica stood and walked out the door, closing it behind her. Renee was left in the dark. She reached over to the bedside table and felt around until her fingers landed on cold metal. It was the small piece of artwork Jeremiah had given her. She couldn't see it in the darkness, but the image was vivid and clear in her mind. It was only two inches tall, with copper and silver encircling each other in what could only be described as an intimate embrace. She ran her thumb along the curves of the design as she thought.

JEREMIAH AND AARON sat at the kitchen table, where they'd been sitting since arriving hours ago. The time had passed in a mix of marriage talk and silence. Jeremiah didn't feel anywhere close to normal, but it was nice to spend a little time with his friend, and to see him so happy.

Aaron stood up with a groan. "It's late. I need to get some sleep. See you tomorrow?"

Jeremiah nodded. "It's a big day. I'll make you a special wedding-day breakfast."

He tried not to think about Renee sitting at this same table, eating the food he'd made for her. She had looked so cute. He stood up, too, though he couldn't imagine trying to sleep with his mind such a jumble.

Aaron seemed to sense his friend's thoughts. "What are you going to do?"

Jeremiah shrugged. "I think I'll go for a walk."

A walk would clear his thoughts. It was worth a shot, at least. Then maybe he'd be able to get some sleep.

Aaron picked up his overnight bag and headed for the stairs. "Don't stay out too late. As the best man, you're not allowed to take a nap during the ceremony. And I expect my breakfast bright and early. You can make it wearing that apron I noticed in the pantry, which looks suspiciously similar—"

"Another word and you won't get your matching hot pads," Jeremiah said, cutting him off.

"Fair enough," Aaron said, disappearing into the hallway.

Jeremiah's lips twitched. Then Aaron was gone and Jeremiah was alone in the big empty kitchen.

He shrugged on his jacket and headed out into the cold dark night, the sky above him bright with stars. He walked down along his property, every tree and building nothing more than dark shapes in the moonlight.

He had lived on this land all his life and could walk it blindfolded. It didn't give him any comfort on this night, though. Wherever he went, Renee was still there. He walked out into the brush, letting the cool air seep under his skin. But nothing helped.

His grandparents had bought the land when they were newlyweds. It had been their dream to own a ranch, and they'd worked it for fifty years, the last thirty as a family business with their grown son and his wife, Jeremiah's parents.

When Jeremiah's grandparents died, his parents moved to Florida, leaving him to keep the land going if he wanted. Now that he looked around, though, he realized that he didn't really enjoy the ranching life. He'd just done it because he couldn't think of anything else to do. And even when he'd found something he truly loved to do, he didn't believe it could be a legitimate vocation.

But why couldn't it? He felt the need for some advice, and it couldn't wait.

He jogged back into the house and up the stairs to the guest room where Aaron was staying and banged on the door. "Aaron, get up. I want to talk to you about something. It's important."

Aaron opened the door, his hair a mess and his eyes bleary. "This better be good."

Jeremiah had been so intent on his own thoughts that he'd forgotten his friend was getting married the next day. "Sorry to wake you, but it'll only take a second. Come on."

Jeremiah led Aaron out to his work shed, Aaron muttering about how late it was the whole way. When Jeremiah opened the door and turned on the lights, though, the grumbling stopped. Aaron stared quietly at the sculptures filling the room. Jeremiah waited.

"You made these?" Aaron asked.

Jeremiah nodded.

Aaron slapped him on the back. "You're an artist. That's cool. You going to sell them?"

"Actually, I was thinking. What if I moved away from the ranch and did this full-time?"

Aaron thought about it for a second. "It would be weird to not have you nearby, but these are good, and if it makes you happy, then you should do that."

Jeremiah felt some of the weight on his chest lift. "So you don't think it's a crazy idea?"

"Way less crazy than waking me up in the middle of the night before my wedding day to show me a bunch of art. I'm going to bed now."

Aaron left, and Jeremiah looked around at his pieces, the possibilities open before him.

He knew he wouldn't be able to sleep, and the warring feelings inside him made his fingers itch. He stepped into the shed and got to work.

RENEE OPENED HER EYES. The sky outside her window was still dark, but she had been tossing and turning for so long that dawn couldn't be that far off. She checked her phone.

It was just a few minutes before five o'clock. She considered trying to go back to sleep, but after a few moments she stood and stretched. There was no point closing her eyes when all she saw was the way Jeremiah's face looked as he'd left her last night. Better to get up and have some coffee, maybe even try to get some more work done—though she had a feeling she knew how that would go.

She opened her door carefully, trying not to make any noise. As she walked down the stairs, she saw light streaming through the kitchen doorway. Someone had beaten her to the punch this morning, it seemed.

Renee entered the kitchen and found Jessica sitting at the table, a mug between her hands. "You're up early. Nervous?" Renee asked her.

Jessica shook her head. "Excited."

Renee got her own mug and sat down beside her sister, who would be getting married in ten hours. Jessica's eyes were sparkling, her cheeks rosy, and a little smile seemed permanently glued to her lips.

Renee couldn't think of a time when she'd felt as happy as her sister looked, except for a few glorious moments in Jeremiah's arms.

Renee tried not to let the heaviness she felt show. It was her sister's wedding day and she was *not* going to ruin it. "It seems like Stew won't ruin your wedding after all, right?"

Jessica sipped her coffee, looking over the rim at her. Renee thought she might return to the conversation topic from the night before, but she didn't. Instead, she rolled her eyes. "Fine, you were right. He's perfectly nice."

Renee tried to feel good about her sister's rare admission of fault, but she couldn't bring herself to gloat. "Is there anything we need to do this morning?"

Jessica nodded. "We need to put the centerpieces on the table and make our bouquets. We've got plenty of time, though."

Renee stood. She needed to feel busy. Idle time led to thinking, and she didn't want to think right now. Not about her job, not about Jeremiah. She went over to the buckets of flowers sitting in the corner of the kitchen and pulled out a handful of roses. "I'll just start getting the thorns off the roses. One less thing to do later."

Before Jessica could comment, her phone buzzed, for which Renee was grateful. She didn't need any lectures right now.

Jessica said, "Good morning, husband-to-be. Why are you up so early?"

He's probably just as excited as she is, Renee thought. She turned and focused on the flowers in her hands. She was happy for them, but that didn't mean she wanted to see Jessica's gooey look again.

"Really? Sculpting? It's weird that he never told us."

Renee smiled. Jeremiah had finally told Aaron about his artwork. When Jessica hung up, she wanted to ask about it, but stopped herself. It wasn't her concern.

That thought killed the smile on her lips and she turned back to the flowers.

"You ready?"

Jeremiah looked down at the rings and nodded.

Aaron fixed his tie one last time. "Don't be nervous."

"You're the one getting married, remember?"

Aaron smiled at the best man. "I've got the easy part. If something happens to those rings, Jessica will kill you."

Jeremiah put the rings inside his breast pocket and patted it. "Safe as can be."

"Then let's get out there."

Jeremiah followed Aaron to the far corner of the barn, where the decorated arch stood, waiting. They took their places and the music changed. Cindy, Jessica's best friend, came down first, with Renee following shortly after. Jeremiah kept his eyes off her, but it didn't stop his heart from pounding. Still, he ignored it and kept thoughts of her and their adventures in the nearby loft out of his head. This was about Aaron and Jessica.

Jeremiah heard Aaron let out a long breath and looked up to see Jessica in the barn doorway. She radiated joy as she walked toward Aaron and married life. Jeremiah couldn't stop himself from glancing at Renee. Her eyes were filled with tears as she watched her sister walk down the aisle.

Jeremiah wasn't sure if he hoped some of those tears were for him.

By the time Jessica had reached Aaron and was holding his hand, Jeremiah had torn his gaze away from the beautiful bridesmaid, determined not to look her way again, no matter how much he wanted to.

RENEE LEANED AGAINST the outer wall of the barn and breathed a sigh of relief. The ceremony had been difficult—forcing herself not to stare at Jeremiah the entire time was one of the hardest things she'd ever had to do, and it felt like her heart was tearing out of her chest the entire time. When Jessica had come down the aisle, the thought of what Renee might have given up made her want to cry.

But she wasn't Meg Ryan, and this wasn't some chick flick where everything worked out. Her life was too different from Jeremiah's, and that was all there was to it. And she was so close to being done with this whole mess. If she could avoid him for a couple more hours during the reception, she would be able to go hide in her room for the rest of the evening. After that, she just needed to sit tight until her flight Sunday morning, and then she'd be home free. For the time being, she would spend her hours looking forward to getting back to New York and going to work on Monday instead of mooning over Jeremiah.

The thought wasn't as appealing as she wanted it to be, but that was all the more reason to get out while she still could. Another day in his arms, losing herself in his eyes, and she wasn't sure she'd be able to leave. But for now, she could and she would, and it was really the best thing.

She didn't need anything but work to make her happy. Really.

Renee was thankfully pulled out of her thoughts by her mother's voice. "Renee! There you are! We have a problem."

At first Renee assumed it was about Stew's orange suit. "Did Jessica say something? Does Stew need to go find a different suit or something?"

By the look on her mom's face and the way she was glancing around as if she was worried someone was listening, Renee knew that whatever was going on was going to be worse than just the suit. She braced herself for something Jessica-freak-out bad.

The older woman didn't keep her in suspense. "There's no cake."

"What?" Renee asked, not sure she had heard correctly. As bad as Renee had guessed it would be, she hadn't imagined it would be *that* bad.

"The cake never showed. I just called the shop, and they lost the order or something, and now there isn't time to make one. You need to tell Jessica that she doesn't have a cake and find out what she wants us to do."

"I have to tell her? Why me?" This was really not Renee's best day ever.

"I know you can break the news to her calmly. Go on, the sooner the better. There isn't much time."

Renee dropped her head back against the wood behind her, then stood up straight. The reception was starting in ten minutes, and she was supposed to tell her sister that there wasn't going to be a cake. How the hell was she going to do that?

Renee forced herself to leave her mother's side and walked over to where Jessica and Aaron were taking pictures. They looked so happy staring into each other's eyes while the photographer's camera clicked over and over again.

Renee waited until there was a lull while the photographer set up for the next shot, then walked over to the happy couple. "So, funny story," she said, but then paused.

She wasn't sure how to say what needed to be said.

"What's going on?" Jessica asked immediately, her eyes narrowing.

Renee froze like a deer in headlights.

"Is it about Stew's suit? I know you tried to hide that from me, but I saw it and I'm okay. Worse things have happened."

Truer words were never spoken.

It was clear Renee wasn't doing a good job of easing into the bad news. At this point it was best to just come out with it. She said it all in a rush, as if that would soften the blow somehow. "The cake never showed, and apparently it's not going to make it."

Jessica's mouth opened into an O of surprise. "There's no cake?" she asked softly.

Aaron put his arm around her and squeezed. Renee felt guilty for some reason and kept talking to fill the silence. "Mom called the shop, and apparently there was an issue and your order wasn't filled. I'm sure you'll get your money back," she finished lamely.

Jessica kept staring at Renee, and Renee quietly waited for the meltdown. Aaron wrapped his arms around his new wife and tugged her close. Once her eyes moved away from Renee and focused on him, he kissed her lightly. "I'm sorry, babe. Tell me what I can do to help fix this so you can be happy on our wedding day."

Jessica's look softened as she stared into her husband's eyes, and Renee's heart, still raw from all it had been through, ached. Jessica took a deep breath and turned to her sister. "We'll survive. Ask Mom to Mac-Gyver something for the cake cutting, but if we can't find anything in time, we'll just do without."

Renee was dumbfounded. Had she heard correctly? "*MacGyver* something?"

Jessica nodded. "You know, pull something together. Preferably using a paper clip and some duct tape." She laughed at her own joke.

Renee couldn't believe this. "I know what it means to MacGyver something, I just don't understand. You're not going to freak out? What about needing everything to be perfect?"

Jessica looked at Aaron again. "Everything *is* perfect, with or without a cake."

Aaron rubbed his hand along her jaw and nodded, and they leaned in for a kiss so passionate it made Renee blush.

When they finally came up for air, Jessica broke away from Aaron, whispering in his ear. He nodded and walked out of earshot.

"We need to talk privately," Jessica told her sister.

Renee felt strangely relieved. "You really are freaking out. You just didn't want Aaron to know."

Jessica shook her head. "Nope. I really don't care about the cake. I'm sure Mom will figure out something that'll be fine." She put her hands on her hips and gave Renee a very big-sister look. "No, I wanted to talk to you alone so you could tell me what's going on with you. You've been mopey for days, and you promised you'd talk to me about it after the wedding. Well, it's after the wedding now. Spill."

"You know I meant later than this."

"Yes, but we have time right now and I want to help my little sister with whatever's going on. Let me help. Start talking."

Renee didn't want to tarnish her sister's wedding day by explaining exactly what she'd been up to that week. Even if Jessica was somehow magically okay with not having a cake, her little sister sleeping with the best man could send her over the edge into full-blown hysteria. Still, Renee needed to talk to somebody she could trust, and Jessica didn't seem like she was about to take no for an answer. Renee took a deep breath and chose her words carefully.

"I've been seeing somebody lately, but things got too serious and I had to break it off. I'm just trying to recover. It's no big deal, really."

"Why did you break it off?"

That was the question Renee had been answering in her mind over and over again. "I can't be in the kind of a relationship he wants. Not with this new job starting."

Jessica shook her head, her curls bouncing elegantly around her shoulders. "No, Renee. It's time you stop hiding behind your job."

Renee was about to argue, but Jessica continued, "Ever since Dad died, you've thrown yourself into your work and distanced yourself from everyone. It's true, so don't argue. I think you're afraid to fall in love and then lose someone."

Renee felt dumbstruck for the second time in less than ten minutes. Was that what she'd been doing? She didn't know for sure, but the idea made her stomach feel queasy. She pushed it to the side to examine later. She grasped for the train of thought Jessica had derailed. "Well, there are other problems. He doesn't live in New York, for one—"

"—and I'm guessing you didn't even talk to him about how to work around that," Jessica interrupted. "Go on, what else?"

Renee sighed, exasperated with her sister's know-it-all attitude. She seemed so sure everything was fixable, but she didn't understand and Renee couldn't explain it without telling her secret. "It's not that easy, Jess. I can't just move and give up my job and everything I am for a guy."

There was a silence as Jessica absorbed what she had said.

"That's what you think I did, isn't it?" Jessica asked, her hands flat against the front of her gown.

Renee didn't answer.

"I didn't give up my identity, Renee," Jessica said, her voice quiet but firm. She put one hand on Renee's arm and looked her straight in the eye, as if trying to get her to listen carefully to what she had to say. "I found a guy and a place that matched my identity. I was never New York. I like animals and trees and jeans, and living here suits me. I was always Texas— I just didn't know it."

Renee looked down at Jessica's hand. The new wedding ring sparkled, and she thought about how happy her sister seemed. Maybe there was a way to have that, too. Jessica continued, "I'm still editing, which I love, but I'm also taking time to be happy and enjoy life with someone I love. That's what's important. Really, the only issue is whether or not you love this guy. If you do, you can figure out the rest of that stuff. You're a smart woman."

Renee didn't know what to say. "I need to go talk to Mom about the cake."

Jessica nodded. "Think about what I said. And don't stress about the cake. You worry too much."

With that, Jessica turned and flounced away in her beautiful wedding dress. Back to taking pictures, back to the man she loved. Renee sighed and went to find her mom and pass on the message to "MacGyver something."

As she walked, she opened her silver clutch purse and pulled out the small metal piece of artwork Jeremiah had given her. She stroked the copper and silver curves, then put it back in her purse just as her mother scurried up.

"Is she okay? What did she say?"

Renee shrugged. "She's fine. She just said to figure something out and that it wasn't a big deal." Her mom looked confused, so Renee added, "She's just happy to be married to Aaron, I guess."

The older woman gave Renee a watery smile. "When I married your dad, I was so happy I wouldn't have noticed if the roof collapsed on top of us."

The thought of how much her dad loved her mom made Renee ache inside. She didn't know what to say.

Stew walked up at that moment in his terrible suit and wrapped his arm around her mother's waist. "Did you speak to Jessica, Gloria?"

Renee watched her mom as she explained about Jessica's reaction, and recognized the look on her face. She loved Stew. Her husband had died and she was willing to love again, even if it meant she might get hurt.

Stew nodded as her mother finished. "You stay here. I think I saw a shop in town that might work. I'll take Aaron's truck and be back in a jiffy."

With that he kissed Renee's mom on the cheek and hustled away. "He's a nice man," Renee said.

Her mom nodded, watching him go.

JEREMIAH FELT WORN-OUT, but he tried not to show it. He hadn't gotten much sleep the night before, and the glare of the lights in the tent was making his head ache. He had a new piece of art to show for his long, sleepless night, at least. It was full of sharp edges and deep cuts.

If he could just get through a few hours of this reception, he'd be free to do whatever he wanted for the next, well, forever. His empty calendar yawned in front of him. He could keep himself busy trying to sell his pieces and figuring out where to go, what to do next.

Jeremiah brought himself back to the present, to the wedding reception going on all around him. He looked down at the paper in front of him again, a frown creasing his brow. In less than an hour, he would need to make his best man speech. The problem was, he'd written it days ago, and it was funny and light and happy, three things he definitely wasn't feeling.

He needed to rewrite it—that was for sure. Although what to say completely eluded him. Still, the idea of changing his speech at least gave him an excuse to slip away from all the merriment and avoid being around all those people. Especially that one person, the woman whom he constantly saw out of the corner of his eye.

He went over to where Aaron sat, looking so damn happy it was annoying, and said, "I'm going to head up to the house for a minute. I need to make some quick tweaks to my speech. I've got time, right?"

Aaron studied his friend for a minute before nodding. "Speeches aren't for a half hour or so. Are you going to tell me what's wrong yet?"

Jeremiah thought for a second, but he already knew the answer. "I will, but not today. For multiple reasons."

Aaron seemed to accept that, and Jeremiah exited the tent and made his way toward Jessica and Aaron's house. Inside, he grabbed a pen and one of Jessica's many pads of paper and sat down on the couch to write, grateful for the silence.

He quickly wrote a new draft of his speech, then ripped off the page and started again as soon as he re-read it. He couldn't read something that fake and generic at Aaron's wedding, but what could he say that was honest without bringing down the whole party?

It would just need to be something sincere. Just because Renee didn't want to be with him didn't make Jessica and Aaron's love any less special. He started writing again.

"Hey, Jeremiah."

The sound of her voice made him jump, sending a squiggle of ink down the page. He turned and looked straight at Renee, something he'd managed to avoid the entire day. God, she looked beautiful in her bridesmaid dress.

She seemed to be waiting for him to say something, but what was he supposed to say? Hi? Good to see you? Remember that time when I told you I loved you and all you could do was shake your head?

Better not to say anything. After a few seconds, she sat down. Her eyes never left his, and he couldn't have pulled his away if he wanted to. She said, "I'm sorry about yesterday. The truth is I'm scared. But I don't want to lose you because—"

She hesitated, and hope rushed through him like a wildfire. He tried to tamp it down, but it was impossible. "Because," he prompted.

"Because I love you, too," she finished, a flush deepening the color of her cheeks.

For a second he wondered if this was a delusion created by too-little sleep. His hand slid up her arm and cupped her cheek. She was real all right.

A giddiness took over, and before he knew what was happening, he leaned in and took her mouth with his, feeling the pleasure of her lips erase all the tension that had built up in his body.

He wanted to laugh, to pick her up and whirl her around, to kiss every inch of her until she came again and again.

He opted for the third one. He'd do the others later, but a man had to have priorities.

Now that she'd said it, the truth of her words left her feeling light and free. She kissed him back enthusiastically, and when they finally broke apart for air, she said them again. "I love you, Jeremiah."

He gave her his wonderful lopsided smile. "What took you so long?"

She shook her head. "I don't know. I was scared. I can be pretty stupid sometimes."

He pushed the hair out of her eyes. "You're wonderful, Renee."

He pulled her closer and his mouth went to her ear. With a nibble at her earlobe that made her shiver with delight, he said, "I love you, too."

Jeremiah's lips and tongue moved slowly down her throat. Renee continued with her prepared speech, even as his touches drove all thoughts from her mind. "You should know I don't care about ranches and horses and chickens."

"Good," Jeremiah answered, his hot breath on the wet trail he'd made causing her to gasp. "I hate chickens. They're horrible devil-beasts."

He slid her down on the couch so he loomed over her, then moved on to teasing her nipples. Even through the dress, his touch made her moan deep in her throat as her nipples hardened into tight nubbins. "What about the ranches and horses?" she managed to get out while she unbuttoned his pants, eager to touch him.

He growled as her fingers grasped his dick, sliding a condom along his length. She had felt silly at first when she'd gone up to her room and grabbed one before searching for Jeremiah, but now she was extremely grateful to her past self. When Jeremiah spoke again, his voice was ragged. "You know, I've never really loved being a rancher. I think I'm going to like living in the city."

Her stomach fluttered at the words. He was going to come to New York to be with her. She still hadn't absorbed the idea that he would leave Texas to be with her.

"We still need to do the Vegas rodeo, though," he added.

She could live with that. "I'll even wear a cowboy hat."

She saw fire dancing in his eyes as his hands roved over her. "I've seen you in a cowboy hat. It's a good look."

He slid her skirt up, revealing her thong. In seconds, it was pushed to the side and his fingers were playing her like a musical instrument. She arched her back against the couch, pulling him fully on top of her. She bit at his lower lip.

He positioned himself against her, making her squirm with delight. "I think I'll spend some time working on my art. Maybe do some shows or something."

She nodded, her eyes closed, nearly all her control gone. She could hardly keep the thread of the conversation going, but there was still more to say. "I'll help you. I'll have more free time, since I'm going to try working only normal hours for a change. Now that I have a reason to be home, it seems like a good time to try to work like a person who has a life outside of the office."

With that, he kissed her deeply as he buried himself inside her, making her cry out with the pleasure of it all. He groaned. "Yeah, I'm definitely going to love New York. It'll be like a movie. *A Cowboy in New York City.*"

She couldn't respond with anything more than his name as he rode her toward oblivion.

After, they rearranged their clothing and went back to the reception, giddy with the emotions of the last half hour. They walked to the tent hand in hand. As they entered, Jeremiah looked at her, as if waiting to see what she would do. Instead of letting go, she squeezed his hand and kept it in hers. "I suppose we should go tell them, now that we're planning on a long-term relationship."

That idea sent a thrill through her, and his wide grin suggested that he felt the same. They strode together toward where Jessica and Aaron sat. Jessica eyed their clasped hands.

Before her sister could say anything, Renee said, "Jessica, remember how you're not freaking out, even when there's no cake?"

Jessica seemed suspicious, but only said, "There's cake. Stew went to a store in town called *Nothing Bundt Cake,* so now we'll be doing a Bundt cake cutting. He saved the day, even if his suit is a bad color."

Renee wanted to comment on the fantastic shop name, but there were more important things to focus on. "Well, you didn't freak out about that, so I'm sure you won't freak out about this, either. Jeremiah and I are a couple."

Jessica rolled her eyes. "Yeah, we know."

"You know?"

"Of course. You two weren't exactly all that good at hiding what was going on," Jessica said, smirking. "I mean, you're really not that subtle. That day you two were putting up the lights, you were making out right next to the door. You really didn't think I saw you? And your footsie under the table bordered on pornographic."

Renee was amazed. "You saw us? And you didn't say anything?"

Jessica shook her head. "Nope. We wanted to give you two a chance to make it happen on your own before stepping in with an added push or two. Remember how I said I owed you for your help with the wedding? Well, now we're even."

A realization swept over Renee and she slapped her

head, feeling incredibly stupid. "There was no burst pipe." It wasn't a question.

Jessica laughed so hard she couldn't speak. Aaron took over, "I was so sure you two would figure that one out and see what we were up to, but Jessica said she could pull it off. I'm still surprised neither of you saw through that. I lost a bet there."

"What did you bet?" Jeremiah asked.

Aaron didn't answer, but his smirk and the way Jessica blushed said it was something inappropriate to discuss in public.

Renee narrowed her eyes. "Wait. If you wanted us to get together enough to come up with a reason to kick me out of your house, and you knew what was going on the whole time, then why did you keep barging in on us?"

Jessica said, "Oh, that was just because it was more fun that way. Watching you two pretend to be innocent and trying to act cool when it was so obvious was absolutely hilarious."

Renee couldn't believe her sister. She'd been set up and had had no idea. Jessica seemed so proud of herself.

Jeremiah wrapped his arm around her waist and turned to the newly married couple. "I'm going to kill both of you, you know that, right?" he said, but his mouth was spread in a wide grin.

Renee smiled, too. They'd been tricked, but she had to admit, it was the best trick of her life.

Jessica stood. "It's time for the cake cutting now. Are you ready to watch us cut a very beautiful last-minute Bundt cake? I'm sure it's going to be delicious."

Jessica looked at them as if daring anyone to disagree.

Nobody did, and everyone watched as Jessica and Aaron sliced into their last-minute cake.

Everyone except for Renee and Jeremiah. They were too busy staring at each other to see anything else.

Epilogue

"I JUST GOT off the phone with the bakery. The cake is now on its way to the reception hall." Jessica said as she strode into the room.

Renee looked at her sister in disbelief. "You called them again? I told you to leave them alone the last time you called a half hour ago."

Jessica looked at herself in the mirror, adjusting her midnight-blue bridesmaid dress so it fell perfectly over her rounded stomach. "I know, but I just wanted to double-check."

"Double-checking was at least five calls ago. At this point I wouldn't be surprised if they didn't deliver my cake out of spite."

"Oh, you'll have cake. They know exactly how important it is that there's cake at your reception. I made it very clear to them."

Renee didn't want to think about what Jessica might have said to the poor woman who owned the bakery. "I'm going to hope they think you're a crazy pregnant lady and don't charge me extra for the annoyance."

Jessica waved her hand in the air, as if it was ridiculous to think that anyone would mind being repeatedly called and threatened over the delivery of a baked good. "I'm your maid of honor. It's my job to make sure everything's perfect."

It really wasn't, but Renee didn't say anything. She had known Jessica would become the ultimate wedding planner before she even asked her sister to be the maid of honor. If she hadn't, she wouldn't be Jessica. So there was nothing she could do but let her sister indulge in some of her more neurotic traits and relax, knowing that everything was in good hands.

"Thanks, Jessica," she said. "I know you've got it under control. Nothing will go wrong, I'm sure."

Jessica was about to respond when her phone buzzed with an incoming text. Worry lines appeared on Jessica's forehead as she read whatever it said, and Renee waited for whatever bad news her sister had gotten. "Did I speak too soon?" she asked.

Jessica looked up and gave the bride a tight smile. "Don't worry. I can take care of this. I'll be back in ten minutes."

With that, she started to rush toward the door. "The ceremony starts in fifteen!" Renee called after her sister, but by the time she finished, the door was already closed and she was alone, wondering what had happened. Whatever it was, she doubted it was anywhere near as bad as Jessica thought it was.

With a few minutes alone in the little bridal room that adjoined the chapel, Renee sank into the couch in the corner, her skirt poufing up as she did so. She chuckled to herself, amazed once more that she'd ended up in a poufy white gown covered in sparkly rhinestones. Who would have guessed?

Someone knocked on the door. She assumed it was her mom, coming to tell her what Jessica was dealing with. "Come in," she called, not moving from her spot.

Jeremiah poked his head into the room. "Is Jessica gone?"

Renee felt a rush of affection as her husband-to-be walked in, a giant smile on his face. "I wanted us to have a couple of minutes alone before the ceremony," he said, sitting beside her on the couch.

She looked him up and down, enjoying the way his suit hugged his body. "You look amazing," she said, reminding herself that she couldn't undress him at that exact moment.

He wrapped an arm around her bare shoulders. "You, too. This is the dress I've heard so much about but wasn't allowed to see, huh? Wow. Worth the wait."

It was only then that she remembered she was in her wedding dress. "You weren't supposed to see me before the ceremony, you know."

He gave her his lopsided grin. "I know. Jessica wouldn't have let me in."

Realization dawned on Renee. "You sent that text." He didn't deny it. "What did you tell her?"

"I said that Aaron couldn't find the boutonnieres."

She glanced at the flower pinned to his breast pocket. "She's going to kill you when she figures out it was a lie."

Jeremiah shrugged. "She can't kill me. It would ruin the wedding, which is her main priority today."

His logic was infallible—she had to give him that. She snuggled closer to him, shoving sections of her dress out of her way to do so. "Another woman asked about my ring this morning. The lady at the hair salon wanted to know if you would be making more of them. I gave her your number."

She glanced down at the delicate golden band wrapped around her left ring finger. The intricate details still amazed her, and she couldn't imagine how much time and work Jeremiah had put into secretly creating it before he proposed. It was truly a thing of beauty.

He squeezed her closer. "I'll think about that after the honeymoon. Right now, there are other things on my mind than building up a new business."

"So you're ready to give up your bachelorhood in about ten minutes and settle down as an old married couple?" she asked, looking up at him.

His eyes roved over her body again, making her skin tingle. "If it means I get to see what you're wearing under this dress later tonight, then absolutely."

She gave him a seductive smile. "Not much."

He leaned in, his lips inches from hers. "My favorite," he whispered, tugging at a loose strand of her hair.

She lost herself in his eyes as he closed the gap between them.

Just as their lips touched, Jessica's voice broke into the moment, forcing them apart. "No! Hair, makeup, dress! You're going to ruin all of it!"

They both looked at the angry pregnant lady towering over them. "You're not even supposed to be in here, Jeremiah. You need to get up to the altar."

She shook her head at him. "Do you have any idea how worried I was when I got your text?"

Renee tried to stifle her laugh at her sister's serious manner, but she couldn't stop herself from giggling. "Jess, you need to calm down. Everything's fine. You've done a great job. Now relax a smidge and let me enjoy my wedding."

Jessica looked as if she might give some sort of a retort, but then she took a deep, calming breath. "Okay. It's your wedding—you do what you want. But Jeremiah, you need to be out of this room in forty-five seconds if we're going to keep to the schedule."

Jeremiah nodded solemnly, but his eyes sparkled. "Thanks for being so relaxed about everything."

Jessica either missed or chose to ignore his sarcasm, because she just smiled and nodded at him.

Renee waited for a second, then realized her sister was going to keep standing there unless she said something. "You might want to turn around if you don't want to watch us making out for the next forty-five seconds."

Jessica rolled her eyes and turned her back. "Thirty-five."

Renee's gaze went to her husband-to-be. "We better make this time count," she said.

He didn't need any more prompting than that, pulling her close and pressing his lips to hers. The world disappeared as she savored the moment.

It took three tries for Jessica to pull them apart. "Okay, now you really are behind schedule," she told them.

Jeremiah leaned his forehead against Renee's as they caught their breath. "Are you ready?"

She smiled up at him. "I am."

He shook his head. "It's 'I do.' You might want to practice before you get up there."

Renee rolled her eyes. "You better get out of here before Jessica has a meltdown. I'll see you in a minute."

He gave her one more kiss, then left.

Renee stood, and Jessica fussed around her for a few moments before declaring everything perfect. Then Jessica handed Renee her bouquet. "Love you, little sis. Let's go get you married."

Renee nodded, unable to speak, and followed her sister out the door. Her heart was too full for words as she walked out to join the man of her dreams.

* * * * *

REQUEST YOUR FREE BOOKS!
2 FREE NOVELS PLUS 2 FREE GIFTS!

H HARLEQUIN®

Blaze®

red-hot reads!

SPECIAL EXCERPT FROM

HARLEQUIN

Blaze

Hannah Hastings is just looking for a hot vacation fling.
Can fun-loving and downright gorgeous rancher
Seth Landers tempt her to stay forever?

Read on for a sneak preview of
SIZZLING SUMMER NIGHTS,
the latest book in Debbi Rawlins's much loved
MADE IN MONTANA *miniseries.*

"I think the best we can hope for is no rocks." Seth nodded to an area where the grass had been flattened.

"This is fine with me," she said, and helped him spread the blanket. "What? No pillows?"

Seth chuckled. "You've lived in Dallas too long."

Crouching, he flattened more of the grass before smoothing the blanket over it. "Here's your pillow, princess."

Hannah laughed. "I was joking," she said, then pinned him with a mock glare. "Princess? Ha. Far from it."

"Come here."

"Don't you mean, come here, please?" She watched a shadow cross his face and realized a cloud had passed over the moon. It made him look a little dangerous, certainly mysterious and too damn sexy. He could've just snapped his fingers and she would've scurried over.

"Please," he said.

She gave a final tug on the blanket, buying herself a few seconds to calm down. "Where do you want me?"

"Right here." He caught her arm and gently pulled her closer, then turned her around and put a hand on her shoulder. "Now, look up. How's this view?"

Hannah felt his heat against her back, the steady presence of his palm cupping her shoulder. "Perfect," she whispered.

His warm breath tickled the side of her neck. He pressed his lips against her skin. "You smell good," he murmured, running his hand down her arm. With his other hand he swept the hair away from her neck. His breath stirred the loose strands at the side of her face.

Hannah was too dizzy to think of one damn thing to say. She saw a pair of eerie, yellowish eyes in the trees, low to the ground. Then a howl split the night. She stifled a shriek, whirled and threw her arms around Seth's neck.

He enfolded her in his strong, muscled arms and held her close. "It's nowhere near us."

"I don't know why it made me jumpy," she said, embarrassed but loving the feel of his hard body flush with hers. "I'm used to coyotes."

"That was a wolf."

Wolf? Did they run from humans or put them on the menu? She leaned back and looked up at him. Before she could question whether or not this was a good idea, Seth lowered his head.

Their lips touched and she was lost in the fog.

Don't miss
SIZZLING SUMMER NIGHTS
by Debbi Rawlins, available March 2017 wherever Harlequin® Blaze® books and ebooks are sold.

www.Harlequin.com

SPECIAL EXCERPT FROM

HQN™

Single mom Harper Maclean has two priorities—raising her son and starting over. Her mysterious new neighbor is charming and sexy, but Diego Torres asks far too many questions...

Enjoy a sneak peek of CALL TO HONOR, the first book in the new SEAL BROTHERHOOD series by Tawny Weber.

Harper stepped outside and froze.

Diego was in his backyard. Barefoot and shirtless, he wore what looked like black pajama bottoms. Kicks, turns, chops and punches flowed in a seamlessly elegant dance.

Shirtless.

She couldn't quite get past that one particular point. But instead of licking her lips, Harper clenched her fists.

She watched him do some sort of flip, feet in the air and his body resting on one hand. Muscles rippled, but he wasn't even breathing hard as he executed an elegant somersault to land feet first on the grass.

Wow.

He had tattoos.

Again, wow.

He had a cross riding low on his hip and something tribal circling his biceps.

Who knew tattoos were so sexy?

Harper's mouth went dry. Her libido, eight years in deep freeze, exploded into lusty flames.

The man was incredible.

Short black hair spiked here and there over a face made for appreciative sighs. Thick brows arched over deep-set eyes, and he had a scar on his chin that glowed in the moonlight.

Harper decided that she'd better get the hell out of there.

But just as she turned to go, she spotted Nathan's baseball.

"You looking for the ball?" His words came low and easy like his smile.

"Yes, my son lost it." She eyed the distance between her and the ball. It wasn't far, but she'd have to skirt awfully close to the man.

"Good yard for working out," he said with a nod of approval. He grabbed the ball, then stopped a couple of feet from her.

"I should get that to Nathan." She cleared her throat, tried a smile. "He's very attached to it."

"The kid's a pistol." His eyes were much too intense as he watched her face.

That's when she realized what she must look like. She'd tossed an oversize T-shirt atop her green yoga bra and leggings. Her hair was pulled into a sloppy ponytail, and she wore no makeup.

"Thanks for finding it."

His eyes not leaving hers, he moved closer.

Close enough that his scent—fresh male with a hint of earthy sweat and clean soap—wrapped around her.

Finally, he placed the ball in her outstretched hand. "Everything okay?"

No. Unable to resist, she said, "Why do you ask?"

"I don't like seeing a beautiful woman in a hurry to get away from me." The shadows did nothing to hide the wicked charm of his smile or the hint of sexual heat in his gaze.

It was the same heat Harper felt sizzling deep in her belly.

Thankfully, the tiny voice in her mind still had enough control to scream, "Danger."

"I'm hurrying because I don't like to leave my son inside alone," she managed to say. "Again, thanks for your help."

And with that, she slipped through the hedge before he could say another word. It wasn't until she was inside the house that she realized she was holding her breath.

What's next in store for Harper, Diego and the SEAL Brotherhood? Find out when CALL TO HONOR by New York Times bestselling author Tawny Weber, goes on sale in February 2017.